The case against Harry Charlton was sir
role as 'investigative journalist' he was a
knowledge of a Top Secret project at th
London, and to have sold this informati
The case rested on three main items: a c
by an independent witness; some very
found in Charlton's flat; and a large une
his bank account.

Antony Maitland's clerk had already
it wasn't until an old (or perhaps it woul
say a very young) friend came into the
was persuaded to change his mind. He st
he doubted Charlton's innocence, and he
the security services when his client mig
of treason.

Then murder was added to treason.

It was obvious that the staff at the lal
to be investigated, particularly those wit
ledge of the project involved. Once again
self acting in the role of detective.

Maitland is many people's favourite l
He is at his best here in the complex unra
appears initially so simple, and spice is add
domestic life by the presence of Sir Nicl
wife, Vera.

THIS FATAL WRIT

Sara Woods

Then all too late I bring this fatal writ,
The complot of this timeless tragedy;
And wonder greatly that man's face can fold
In pleasing smiles such murderous tyranny.

Titus Andronicus, Act II, scene iii

ISBN: 0 333 25963 7

First published 1979 by
MACMILLAN LONDON LIMITED
4 Little Essex Street London WC2R 3LF
and Basingstoke
Associated companies in Delhi Dublin Hong Kong
Johannesburg Lagos Melbourne New York Singapore
and Tokyo

Printed in Great Britain by
THE ANCHOR PRESS LTD
Tiptree, Essex

Bound in Great Britain by
WM BRENDON & SON LTD
Tiptree, Essex

Any work of fiction whose characters were of uniform
excellence would rightly be condemned – by that fact if
by no other – as being incredibly dull. Therefore no
excuse can be considered necessary for the villainy or
folly of the people appearing in this book. It seems
extremely unlikely that any one of them should resemble
a real person, alive or dead. Any such resemblance is
completely unintentional and without malice.

S.W.

I

'I have some reason to trust you, Mr Maitland,' said Sir Leonard Bowling in his precise way; and considering what had transpired the last time they met in court that was an admission verging on the magnanimous. 'So naturally, when this distressing business came up, I thought of you.'

'Naturally.' If there was a hint of dryness in Antony Maitland's tone, it was not too apparent. 'I believe, however, you heard from Mallory – '

'Bellerby told me your clerk had refused the brief.' Sir Leonard's tone set that aside as of little account. 'I thought perhaps, if I saw you myself . . . and you aren't a man, I take it, to be offended by an unorthodox approach.'

'Hardly.' Maitland's amusement was a little more evident now. 'I've seen what the papers had to say about the matter, yours included.' And that was the trouble, of course, it was something he had no desire to be mixed up in. Still, he liked what he knew of Sir Leonard, was even to some extent obliged to him; better not send him away unheard. 'If you could give me a little more detail,' he added encouragingly, and was immediately assailed by a doubt as to the fitness of offering any such incentive.

'As far as I'm concerned, it all came up out of a clear sky when Charlton was arrested.'

'He's being charged under the Official Secrets Act.' Maitland sounded thoughtful.

'That's right, and I still don't know precisely . . . but that's beside the point.' Sir Leonard, the owner and publisher of *The Courier*, was a man well used to getting his own way, and there could be no doubt that his ignorance in this instance left him feeling aggrieved. 'All I do know is that it concerns some Top Secret project at the Fenton Laboratory. Charlton, who I'm told is a good investigative reporter – they will tag these labels on to people nowadays, at one time that would have been taken for granted – Charlton, I was saying, got hold of some item of information from one of the technicians, and is alleged to have passed it on to a friend of his attached to the Russian Embassy.'

'I thought all the subversive elements there had been weeded out. Over a hundred of them were expelled last month, according to the account I read.'

'One hundred and five,' said Sir Leonard, still precise. 'But I don't for a moment think either of us is so naïve as to believe there wouldn't be others to take their place.' Maitland made no comment on that, just nodded his agreement. 'Anyway, there it is. This fellow is a third secretary or something, nothing very important, no reason why Charlton shouldn't have made a friend of him. Only now it's awkward, you see.'

'I do indeed.' Jenny Maitland would have said he was wearing his 'm'lud, I object,' expression, and certainly her husband, who could find amusement in most things and had started out by taking the matter lightly, was finding as the interview progressed nothing humorous in the situation at all. 'Charlton,' he said now. 'Harry Charlton, isn't it? Do you know him well?'

'I know him by sight, of course. I know him to say "good morning" to. I've had good reports of his ability. Nothing more than that.'

'At least, then, you're not going to tell me, "he wouldn't do a thing like that",' said Maitland hopefully.

'No, though he himself insists – ' But he was interrupted there by Maitland, who said flatly:

'Then I don't quite see – forgive me – what your interest is in the matter.'

'He's an employee, I feel a certain responsibility.'

'But if he's really been selling secrets to the Russians – '

'That has not been proved.'

'Not yet. He admits he had this . . . information?'

'So I understand.'

'But still you think he's innocent?''

Sir Leonard made an oddly indecisive gesture. 'I don't know,' he admitted. 'But I very much hope . . . frankly, Mr Maitland, I don't want another scandal. It's only a few months since Laurence was convicted.'

'Yes, he was a *Courier* man too, wasn't he?' (A fact he very well remembered.) 'But the cases are so very different, nobody's going to make the connection.'

'Don't you think so?' It was strange, in all the circumstances, that he could speak of the affair so lightly. Well, perhaps not lightly exactly, but almost casually. Not quite a year since Lady Bowling – the beautiful Lady Bowling, as the newspapers inevitably described her, and this time with some truth – was brutally strangled and dumped from a car in a side street near Covent Garden. But Sir Leonard, he knew, was a man with a strong sense of duty and capable, in a good cause, of disregarding his own feelings to a quite uncanny degree. The question was, of course, how good was his cause in the present instance? Somehow Maitland doubted . . .

'If the chap really has been peddling secrets – ' he said, very much as he had said before, and let the sentence remain uncompleted. And then, as his companion made no further protest, 'Mallory has already refused the brief, hasn't he? Frankly, I don't feel inclined to reverse the decision.'

'I was afraid of that.' Sir Leonard sounded resigned, but he wasn't finished yet. 'You, of all people, won't tell me that the police never make mistakes.' And that, though he couldn't know it, was nearer the bone than Maitland liked.

All the same, he answered with very little change of tone. 'No, I won't tell you that, though I imagine this is the Special Branch, don't you? But it would be difficult, almost impossible, to make an independent investigation, and once I'd done so I might find myself committed to a client I believed guilty. And of this particular offence – ' He broke off there, and this time Sir Leonard leaped into the conversational gap with something like enthusiasm.

'Take the brief, work to Bellerby's instructions. You needn't do more than that.'

Maitland smiled. 'You're asking me to get him off, guilty or innocent.'

'Well – '

'I don't suppose you've thought it out quite so clearly as that, but that's what it amounts to. I don't know what sort of a case the defence has got – '

'Bellerby seems worried.'

' – but if it's an advocate you want I could name you half a dozen men far more eloquent than I.'

'Bellerby said – '

'I know. He has a phrase he uses when he wants me to get into something "way over my head". He talks about my "special talents"; my uncle is blunter, he calls it meddling. But under either name I don't feel inclined to get involved in this instance.'

Perhaps it was the finality in his tone that convinced his visitor. Sir Leonard got to his feet slowly, Maitland with more alacrity. 'It's the hint of treachery that bothers you, isn't it?' said Bowling. 'Yet I seem to remember that once before you were involved in a treason trial.'

'That was . . . quite different.' But he didn't like the reminder, there had been some heartache about that case before it was over. 'The defence to start with was mistaken identity, and by the time its nature changed I'd come to believe what my client had to say about himself. But I don't know Harry Charlton.'

'And you don't want to,' said Sir Leonard ruefully; an uncanny echo of what Maitland would like to have said if a certain regard for the conventions hadn't stopped him. 'Well, it can't be helped, I suppose.'

'Talk to Bellerby again,' Maitland urged, coming round the desk, 'he's bound to have somebody in mind.'

'I'll do that.' Sir Leonard began to move towards the door.

'I'm grateful to you for giving me so much of your time, Mr Maitland.'

Antony went with him to the door of chambers and watched him for a moment until he disappeared round a bend in the staircase: an erect, grey-haired figure, almost obsessively neat in his dress. It was a pity not to be able to oblige him, but Maitland found in himself no ambition at all to get involved in Harry Charlton's affairs.

Returning, he made for his uncle's room. 'Can you tell me, Uncle Nick, why does Mallory always insist on my taking on matters I've no time for?'

'If you want to enough, you can make time for anything,' said Sir Nicholas Harding, sitting back in his chair and removing his spectacles.

'I didn't mean that, I meant – '

'I know. You were speaking colloquially, as you so often do.' Sir Nicholas sighed, as though all the troubles of the world had suddenly come to rest on his shoulders. 'What is it this time?'

'Bellerby's brief on behalf of that journalist. Mallory said "no", but he can't have sounded as if he meant it, because I've just had Sir Leonard Bowling here badgering me to take it on after all.'

'I cannot believe that Sir Leonard's approach would have been anything but dignified.' Sir Nicholas, recently returned from a protracted honeymoon in Switzerland and in his person almost as neat as the recent visitor, had already reduced the papers on his desk to a shambles. Now he picked a document on stiff blue paper from a so-far-untouched pile, looked at it with every appearance of intelligence for a moment, and then added it to the confusion on his blotting pad. His nephew, who had a casual manner and preferred, when not professionally engaged, a casual style of dress, resisted the temptation to replace it where it came from and said, as though unwillingly:

'He was everything of the most correct.'

'He may have felt you owed him some special consideration.'

9

'He did me a favour, that's true, but – damn it all! – he wanted to know who murdered his wife as much as I did.'

'Probably more,' Sir Nicholas admitted. 'I take it you are telling me you refused his request.'

'I did.'

'Are you really so busy?'

'It could have been fitted in. Mallory pointed that out to me in no uncertain terms.'

'What is it then that makes the matter so distasteful to you?'

'One of his reporters has stumbled on something on the secret list, and passed it on to a pal in the Russian Embassy.'

'Then I must congratulate you, for once, on your strength of mind,' said Sir Nicholas cordially. 'Let us celebrate by going home at once, my dear boy. I believe that Jenny is expecting Vera and myself, as well as you, for dinner.'

'It's Tuesday,' said Antony simply. It would take more than his uncle's marriage to alter a tradition that had been established for many years. 'And if I'm not mistaken we'll find Vera upstairs already,' he added. 'I'll just get my coat.'

II

Antony Maitland could be sober enough in court, but it is undeniable that a charge of behaving, all too frequently, in an unorthodox fashion could quite fairly be levelled against him, as Sir Leonard Bowling had come close to doing that afternoon. And anyone wanting to substantiate such a charge could also have pointed out that the household in Kempenfeldt Square was in some respects an unusual one.

The arrangement had seemed quite logical when it started soon after Antony's demobilisation. The house belonged to Sir Nicholas Harding, as it had belonged to his father and grandfather before him, and accommodation being at that time at a premium the two top floors had been adapted to provide separate living quarters for Antony and his wife, Jenny. But time had proved this temporary expedient to be a convenient, even a pleasant one, and though there were occasions when Antony would have denied this he would have been the first to admit that if there were battles to be fought it might be considered desirable to skirmish on one's own ground. Gradually the strict procedural rules with which they had started were forgotten, so that Sir Nicholas was quite likely to be found taking refuge upstairs when his own domestic arrangements became too much for him, and Maitland was in the habit of borrowing his uncle's study for such conferences as overflowed the normal working day and were more conveniently held at home.

And now, for the first time, an element of change had been introduced. To everyone's surprise but Jenny's, Sir Nicholas had married, at the end of the Trinity term, Miss Vera Langhorne, barrister-at-law, of Chedcombe and the West Midland Circuit. Both Antony and Jenny knew the new Lady Harding well and were fond of her, but whereas Jenny was blithely optimistic about the new ménage, Antony had his moments of doubt. He knew Vera liked him, even trusted him up to a point, but there had been times in the past when he felt she didn't altogether approve of him.

That wasn't on his mind, however, as he followed Sir Nicholas up the steps and into the hall of number five. He was anticipating a pleasantly relaxed evening, with nothing on his list urgent enough to drag his attention away from the music that would no doubt be played and the description of the Hardings' journeyings that would certainly intersperse it.

Gibbs was, as usual, at the back of the hall. It was uncanny how he always managed to be on hand to observe any comings and goings. Gibbs was Sir Nicholas's butler, a cross-grained old man who ought to have retired years ago (his employer would have been only too happy to have eased his path), but who enjoyed making a martyrdom of his continued service.

Antony and Jenny had been in some hopes that he would give in his notice in a dudgeon upon hearing of Sir Nicholas's marriage, but – wonder of wonders – he actually seemed to be pleased about it. So now he said, with something as near to amiability as he was capable of, 'Lady Harding asked me to tell you, Sir Nicholas, that you would find her with Mrs Maitland when you came in.'

'Thank you, Gibbs.' Sir Nicholas shrugged out of his raincoat and handed it over. He was at the foot of the stairs and his nephew was close behind him when the old man spoke again. 'Mr Maitland.' His tone was sharper now. 'There is a young lady to see you.' He made it sound as if he suspected a liaison conducted thus improbably under his employer's roof. 'Miss Canning,' he went on. 'I took the liberty of asking her to wait in the study.'

'Clare?' said Antony, halting abruptly. 'You know her well enough, Gibbs. Why didn't you send her upstairs?'

'Pardon me, Mr Maitland, it was at Miss Canning's own request,' said Gibbs firmly. 'A matter of business, she *said* it was.' His doubts about the truth of the statement could not have been more clearly expressed.

'Well, never mind. You go ahead, Uncle Nick. I'll bring her up with me when I've found out what this is all about.' He wasn't worried as he crossed the hall. He still thought of Clare as a child, and didn't think anything very terrible could be troubling her.

The study still had its vacation-time tidiness. It was a big room with a desk near the window, deep leather chairs with a matching sofa, and a glass-fronted bookcase along the wall opposite the fire. Clare Canning, who knew Sir Nicholas well and wasn't likely to be daunted by his favourite room, was unexpectedly perched on the edge of one of the chairs. She was nineteen now and a stranger would have seen nothing of the child about her, only a spectacularly beautiful young woman with fine, straight hair, naturally blonde, cut short and feathery, eyes of a very deep blue, and enchantingly regular features. But though all that passed Maitland by, as being too familiar for comment, he saw at once that she was troubled. There was something in her expression that took him back

12

eight years to the corridor outside the number one court at the Old Bailey: a pinched look, as though the evening was cold, and a sense of purpose about her that meant that, for better or worse, she had made up her mind to some course of action.

She had got to her feet as he came in and now, hardly waiting for him to shut the door, she came across the room to meet him. 'You're the only person,' she said, and because he knew her so well he acquitted her of over-dramatising whatever the situation was, 'who can help us.'

He had started to say, 'Hallo, Clare,' but broke off in view of the urgency in her tone. 'Take it easy,' he said, taking her hands in his and beginning to lead her back to her chair again. And then, 'Is it cold in here? You're freezing.'

'That doesn't matter.' She waved the question aside impatiently. 'Mr Maitland, I've got to make you understand – '

'All in good time.' He had released her hands and was feeling along the mantelpiece for the box of Swan Vestas that ought to be there, but on this occasion was hiding behind the clock. 'I'll put a match to the fire, shall I? We'll soon have you warm. How is your father keeping . . . and Emmie? And what have you been doing with yourself? We haven't seen you since you left the Art School last year.'

'They're all right, I suppose. I . . . I haven't seen them for a week or two.' The hint of reluctance in Clare's tone was also uncharacteristic. 'I'm not living at Wood Green any more.'

'Your own place? Well, you said you needed a studio.' He was remembering as he spoke that her mother's death had left Clare, even by today's standards, a wealthy young woman.

'In a way,' she said, and now there was no doubt about it at all, she sounded evasive. And that wasn't like Clare either, he had always found her almost transparently honest in her dealings with him.

The fire had responded readily and was already showing a blaze. He moved a little to the side of the hearth, though there was still no heat in the flames, and stood looking down at her. Maitland was a tall man, with dark hair, a pleasantly casual

13

manner, and a humorous look about the eyes that just now was overlaid by anxiety. Obviously idle chatter wasn't going to have a calming effect, he'd better change his tactics and find out what the trouble was. He wanted to help her, that went without saying, but at the same time some sixth sense was warning him that there might be breakers ahead. 'All right, Clare,' he said; and because to the whole household at Kempenfeldt Square Clare was a very special person there was no hint of resignation in his voice. 'Let's have it.'

'It's Harry,' she said, as though that ought to explain everything.

'Wait a bit!' Unintentionally his tone had sharpened. 'You don't mean . . . Harry Charlton?' He didn't like coincidences, but surely it would be an even bigger one if he should be consulted about two men called Harry on the same afternoon.

'Of course I do, why shouldn't I?' She was on the defensive now, and he answered quickly and as soothingly as he could.

'I was surprised, that's all. Sir Leonard Bowling was talking to me about him earlier today.'

'Sir Leonard?' She was frowning now; a thing he realised, as he watched her, that she very rarely did. 'I didn't think he even knew Harry was alive.'

'He knows that all right.' No need to explain Bowling's motives any further.

'Then you know what's happened.'

'The merest outline only.'

'Did Sir Leonard . . . did he really want you to help Harry? Then everything's all right.' She looked for the moment almost like herself again.

'Don't go so fast.' This was going to be difficult, and the devil of it was he wasn't quite sure where the difficulty lay. 'A solicitor called Bellerby – '

'I made Harry go to him. He was Auntie Barbara's solicitor.'

'So he was. I'd forgotten that. Anyway, he offered Mallory a brief for me, but I declined it.'

'Oh, Mr Maitland!' Even a stranger would have seen at

14

that moment a good deal of the child in her. 'But why were you talking to Sir Leonard then? I don't understand.'

'It's quite simple really. He wanted me to change my mind.'

'And you will! Say you will, after all!'

'I'm sorry, Clare.'

'You told him you wouldn't.' That was said with quiet despair, but she wasn't through with him yet. 'If you'd only listen – '

'I'll listen, of course. But before we go any further I'd like to know, what is your interest in this Harry Charlton?'

He could rely on Clare not to be coy with him, and she wasn't. 'We're in love with each other,' she told him, and that was plain enough, but still he had the feeling there was something she was keeping to herself, so that he persisted with his questions beyond the point at which he would normally have felt enough had been said.

'You're engaged to be married to him?' he asked, and now there was something definitely shifty about her, little as the word suited what he knew of Clare.

'Not exactly,' she said, her eyes not meeting his.

'An understanding then.' More appropriate really; after all, Clare was still very young. He pulled himself up on the thought; after all, Jenny had been younger than that when they had married, a foolish business, but sometimes foolishness paid off. But we had the war to mature us, while these children . . .

'I'd better tell you,' said Clare, with desperate honesty. 'We're living together.'

He was too used to the cut and thrust of his work in the courts to show any emotion, though his affection for the girl and the baldness of the statement combined to shake him. Instead he asked, almost casually, 'How old is Harry Charlton?'

'Twenty-seven. I know what you're thinking,' said Clare, and oddly enough she was right about that. 'You're thinking he's older, he's taking advantage of me.' Her tone was scornful now. 'It isn't like that at all.'

15

Her earnestness was disarming. He turned away from her deliberately, seated himself in the chair that was usually his uncle's, and then, trying again to meet her eyes, asked gently, 'How is it then?'

'He asked me to marry him, all very proper.' She sounded absurdly indulgent, as if she were discussing the vagaries of a child. 'It was I who wouldn't.'

'Because you're not sure.' It was more a statement than a question.

'Of course I'm sure.' She smiled at him suddenly, to his relief; he didn't like the intensity she had been showing. 'You've known me too long, Mr Maitland. You still think I'm eleven years old.'

'I wouldn't presume to criticise your decision,' he told her seriously, 'if I was sure you were altogether happy about it yourself.'

She ignored that. 'It's not because I'm not sure of my own mind,' she said again. And added, in a strange echo of his own thought, 'Jenny was younger than I am, wasn't she? And it's lasted between you – hasn't it? – all these years.'

He couldn't resist a smile at that, and wondered immediately whether his amusement would disturb the delicate balance of her confidence. 'You're making me feel my age,' he said lightly.

'Well, you were making me feel mine,' she retorted. 'So that's fair, isn't it? And you still want to know why, and I don't know if I can explain it to you. But the thing is, you see, I don't think I believe in marriage. It's lasted for you and Jenny, but I don't think that's *because* you're married.'

'In spite of it perhaps.'

'You're laughing at me, Mr Maitland.' She paused there, but when he made no comment went on, and now it seemed as if she found the words with difficulty, 'I wouldn't say – would you? – that my parents were an awfully good example.'

'But – ' said Maitland, and stopped. Point out to her that her father's second marriage, though to an outsider it appeared pretty humdrum, had worked out well? Point out that the

16

Auntie Barbara she had mentioned gave every evidence of being rapturously happy with her husband, Derek Stringer, despite all the difficulties he had foreseen for two people of such differing temperaments? He couldn't afford, at this juncture, to forfeit whatever confidence she had in him. He wasn't sure where her story was heading, but he didn't like the situation and could only be thankful she had turned to him.

Clare shook her head energetically at him. 'There aren't any "buts",' she insisted. 'We've been together for four months now, and everything was perfect until all this happened.'

'You'd better tell me.'

'I expect you know as much as I do. He was arrested a week ago, and there's been one hearing in court – '

'The Magistrates' Court,' he amplified.

'Yes, well, that's all really.'

'He was remanded for trial, I suppose. Is he still in custody?'

'No, thank goodness.'

'Do you know what bail was set?'

'He didn't tell me.'

'Or whether the prosecution made any objection to his being released?'

'I don't know that either.'

'I see. Charlton doesn't know you're here?'

'No, I thought . . . he might not like asking help from a stranger. I mean, it would be different if you'd accepted the brief in the first place.'

'So that if you persuade me . . . I don't think you're going to persuade me, Clare.'

She didn't protest at that, as he had expected. Instead, 'Why not?' she demanded.

To tell her he just didn't like journalists wouldn't be tactful. To give her the more pressing reason for his refusal would have to be carefully worded. 'It isn't my kind of case,' he said, and knew as he spoke that he'd have to do better than that to convince her.

'Harry told me you once defended someone in a treason

trial. That was when Mr Bellerby first suggested your name,' said Clare. She didn't say it argumentatively, just as a plain statement of fact.

'That was different,' said Maitland lamely.

'Because you thought your client – whoever he was – was innocent. That's it, isn't it? You've made up your mind Harry's guilty.'

'A lot of my clients are guilty, Clare.' Which was true, as far as it went.

'Yes, I dare say.' She brushed the statement aside. 'It's the treason, isn't it? Because that's what they mean, in spite of this Official Secrets stuff.' He was astonished at the tenacity with which she stuck to her point.

'Clare, it isn't a barrister's business to make up his mind whether his clients are guilty or not. He acts on instructions – '

'But that isn't always true of you.' He had nothing to say to that, and after a moment she went on. 'Mr Maitland, if I swear to you he's innocent will you help us?'

Antony still didn't speak. Instead he got up, skirted the desk, and walked to the window where the heavy velvet curtains were still undrawn. There wasn't much prospect from this room, just a narrow strip of garden with a high wall beyond, but he stood there looking out as though he was fascinated by what he saw. Clare didn't try to interrupt him now, and he was thankful for that; because even with what he knew of her it wasn't an easy decision to make. If he was to believe her, he had no choice but to accede to her request. He wasn't the sort of man whose nature permitted him to pass by on the other side. And even if he didn't find her statement completely convincing, could he refuse to help her? But he would be committing himself to far more than the normal acceptance of a brief, he would be offering to use what that amiable solicitor, Mr Bellerby, called his special talents in an active search for some alternative to Harry Charlton's guilt. And he didn't know Charlton, he didn't want to get involved.

He turned at last. 'You're probably the only person in the world I'd take a statement like that from, Clare,' he said. And again his tone was light, he didn't want her to know how much the decision had cost him. Though, being Clare, she would probably guess anyway.

She got up too, but slowly, as though any sudden movement might cause him to change his mind. 'You do mean it, don't you?' she asked. And then, when he made no answer, but only nodded abruptly, added naïvely, 'I wonder why.'

He smiled at that, and this time the smile was a reminiscent one. 'You accused me just now of treating you as if you were still a child,' he said. 'Do you remember telling me once that if you wanted to paint people you'd got to see them as they really were, not as you'd like them to be? I'm giving you credit for being sufficiently dispassionate to look at Harry with a painter's eye.'

Again Clare had a frown for that. 'I have painted him, of course,' she said slowly. Then the frown disappeared and she smiled in her turn. 'I'm glad you believe me, Mr Maitland, because I'm quite, quite sure.'

III

Twenty minutes later he had taken Clare to the corner of Avery Street to find a cab, returned to the house under Gibbs's disapproving eye, and was on his way up to his own quarters. He went slowly, still not regretting his decision, but wondering how best to break it to his uncle. Because it wasn't going to be a popular one, he was sure of that. But some explanation of Clare's visit would have to be made without delay, and Sir Nicholas being a man of uncertain temper there was always the possibility of a row developing. Which he could have faced with equanimity, for so many years now he and Jenny had been used to coping with the older man's moods; but today there was an added factor to the equation, Vera's presence, and he wasn't quite sure what difference that would make.

Jenny came into the upstairs hall to meet him. She didn't always do that when visitors were present, but obviously she was expecting Clare to be with him. 'Where is she?' she demanded.

'She sent her love to you, but she hadn't time to come up. She had an appointment.'

'Antony, you know that doesn't explain anything,' said Jenny, half exasperated, half amused. 'When Uncle Nick told me – '

'Something rather queer, love.' He was urging her towards the living-room door as he spoke. 'But it touches on a matter Uncle Nick and I were discussing, so I'll have to explain to him too.'

'All right.' She went before him into the room. 'I'll give you a drink, then you can tell us.'

Sir Nicholas was occupying his usual place, the wing chair facing the window; a man as tall as his nephew, fair enough so that what grey there was in his hair was hardly visible. The newspapers, in describing him, were far too apt to use the word 'handsome', which had the worst effect on his temper. Now he was stretched out at his ease, so that Antony thought undutifully, 'a child could play with him', but he wasn't under any illusion . . . the relaxed mood could change in an instant.

Vera, Lady Harding, was sitting at the end of the sofa nearest her husband. For some reason Antony's mind went back to the first sight he had had of her, seven years ago, a tall, heavily-built woman with dark hair liberally streaked with grey, wearing a sack-like beige suit, and hurrying down the steps of the Shire Hall in Chedcombe to catch him before he got too far on his way back to the hotel. Now he was surprised – so surprised that he was almost guilty of staring – to see her wearing a dress that, although still sack-like – a well-cut sack, perhaps – was made of a soft, moss-green material. He had never seen her in anything but what are known as 'neutral' shades before, and the change was so striking that he was almost relieved to see her thick hair beginning to escape from the confining pins.

Jenny went across to the writing-table to pour sherry. Vera smiled without speaking; she had rather a grim smile, of which he had once been somewhat in awe. Sir Nicholas said lazily, 'You ought to know by now, my dear boy, that Gibbs disapproves of damsels in distress.'

Maitland had taken up his favourite place on the hearth-rug, a little to one side of the fire. He said, rather formally, 'I'm sorry I was delayed, Vera.' It would still have felt less strange to be calling her Miss Langhorne. And then, to his uncle, 'How did you know?'

'Clare is a friendly little thing,' said Sir Nicholas. 'I cannot think she was deliberately avoiding us.'

'She wasn't, of course.' He accepted his sherry with a brief word of thanks, and placed the glass next to the clock. 'It was just that it was something it would be easier to tell to one person alone.'

Jenny had curled up at the other end of the sofa. 'If you think that explains anything,' she said. And added, suddenly anxious, 'Is anything wrong?'

'Not with Clare herself. With her . . . her boy friend,' Antony told her, with an amused eye for Sir Nicholas's reaction to the description, which was to close his eyes for a moment as though in pain. 'Rather a coincidence, Uncle Nick,' he went on. 'It's the Harry Charlton I was talking to you about earlier this afternoon.'

Sir Nicholas was suddenly very still. 'The object of Sir Leonard Bowling's solicitude? You will remember, Antony, that I was able to congratulate you, for once, on your good sense in refusing the brief.'

Jenny exchanged a look with Vera. 'You're not telling us,' she protested. Maitland, who had been concentrating on his uncle's reactions, turned instead to look at his wife.

'Harry Charlton is a journalist who has been charged under the Official Secrets Act. Mallory turned down the brief on my behalf – '

'But, Antony, you say that Clare . . . I suppose she's in love with him,' said Jenny tragically.

'I'm afraid she is.'

'And you,' said Sir Nicholas, in the gentle tone that spelled trouble, 'have so far gone back on your word as to say you will see the man.'

Antony hesitated. The room was warm and friendly, with the tranquil air that he would have been the first to admit was entirely Jenny's doing. And surely they could have had the first evening of what might be called the transition period in peace. But it was no good, they were all waiting for his answer, the two women a little puzzled because between uncle and nephew there was only too obviously a sense of strain. 'I did more than that, sir,' Maitland said at last, deliberately. 'I said I'd take the brief.'

Sir Nicholas, who had looked a moment before as if nothing could move him, sat up straight at that. 'Do I understand you?' he enquired. 'You have persuaded yourself somehow of this man Charlton's innocence. And don't tell me,' he commanded, as his nephew started to speak, 'that your clients aren't necessarily innocent of the crimes with which they are charged. Because in this case – '

'You're right, of course, I wouldn't have touched it on any other terms. But I didn't persuade myself, Clare persuaded me.'

'Without your even seeing the man. You wanted to believe her,' said Sir Nicholas accusingly.

And that was true enough, though he was damned if he was going to admit it. 'If it had been anyone but Clare – '

'You're crediting the child with clairvoyance,' said Sir Nicholas, dismissing the argument before it could get off the ground. None of them thought for a moment that he had intended a pun.

'No, I see what Antony means,' said Jenny unexpectedly. 'She has a seeing eye. Well, I know that sounds like one of those dogs,' she added when Sir Nicholas looked back at her blankly. 'But you know what I mean.'

'Do I?' queried Sir Nicholas, and as quickly as it had arisen dropped his grievance. 'You will be wondering what we are talking about, my dear,' he said to Vera. 'Perhaps you would care to explain, Antony.'

22

Maitland, who hated explanations at any time, settled himself to this one with as good grace as he could muster. 'Clare Canning was a witness for the defence in one of Uncle Nick's cases when she was only eleven years old.'

'A matter in which you also played a part,' said Sir Nicholas, setting the record straight.

'Meddling,' Antony agreed. He would never have admitted it, but there were times when the accusation rankled. Still, he was feeling more cheerful now. 'At your express request.' He paused a moment, to let that sink in. 'And that's really all there is to it,' he concluded.

Sir Nicholas turned to Vera again. 'I cannot feel that this explanation will have wearied you too much,' he remarked sarcastically. Antony had a retort ready for that, but Vera forestalled him.

'Told me about the matter yourself,' she reminded her husband. She was at any time a woman of few words, and when she did speak it was generally in a sort of shorthand of her own. 'Day we came up in the train together from Northdean. Didn't remember the child's name, of course, but you said she was an artist with a gift for taking a likeness and with already more penetration of her subject's mind than was good for her.'

'That's exactly what I meant,' said Maitland with some relief. 'That sketch she did of Uncle Nick, now – '

'In which you also appear,' said Sir Nicholas, but apparently without malice.

'Jenny had it framed and it's in the bedroom. You've only to look at that – '

'I am not quite sure what aspect of my character you feel is portrayed there,' said his uncle with interest.

'It was the fact that she'd caught the likeness between the two of you that made it so remarkable,' said Jenny. 'Because you're not really at all alike, you know, except sometimes.'

'I have much to be thankful for,' said Sir Nicholas seriously.

Jenny might have taken him up on that, but she had got to her feet and was making for the door. 'Dinner must be ready by now,' she said over her shoulder. 'I won't be long.'

As soon as the door had closed behind her, Sir Nicholas put down his glass and fixed his nephew with an accusing stare. 'Now, Antony!' he said.

'Now, Uncle Nick?' But he had thought the battle was over, at least for that evening, and wasn't best pleased to find he had been wrong.

'You know perfectly well what I mean. I don't want to worry Jenny – '

'Let me t-take care of that, sir.'

Both his companions knew that the slight stammer meant he was losing his temper. Vera looked worried, but for once Sir Nicholas ignored the fact. 'If I could rely on you to show the least good sense in managing your own affairs!' he said caustically.

'I – '

For the moment they had both of them forgotten Vera, but now she leaned forward, interrupting whatever Antony had been about to say. 'Nicholas,' she said. Her husband looked at her a little wildly, rather as though he couldn't think for the moment who she was, but when she smiled at him his expression softened. 'Don't quite see why you should be so anxious,' she told him.

'Anxious? I am not *anxious*,' said Sir Nicholas, revolted by the suggestion. 'Appalled, if you like. Outraged at such a lack of elementary prudence. But anxious . . . why should I be?'

'You said, on Jenny's account.'

'Well . . . perhaps. If you will permit me to explain . . . or rather, Antony shall do it for me.' He turned again to his nephew, who had been listening to this exchange with some uneasiness. 'You know what you have committed yourself to. You won't tell me you're proposing to follow Bellerby's instructions and take no part in any investigation yourself.'

'In the circumstances, Uncle Nick – '

Sir Nicholas chose to take that as agreement. '*If* Charlton is innocent, of which I am by no means persuaded – '

'We neither of us know much about the matter yet,' Maitland protested. Sir Nicholas pounced on the admission.

'That's just what I'm complaining of. You've made up your mind on no evidence at all – '

'Clare would know if he were the kind of man to do such a thing,' said Maitland stubbornly. His uncle gave a sigh, expressive, more than anything else, of extreme exasperation.

'That I should live to hear any member of my chambers say such a thing,' he said. 'My dear, you will agree with me – '

Vera smiled again her rather grim smile, dividing it impartially between them. 'You haven't told me yet why you are . . . outraged,' she said. It occurred to Antony suddenly that she was laughing at his uncle, which he hadn't, quite frankly, believed her capable of. And Uncle Nick actually liked it, that was even more astonishing. The realisation both startled and pleased him, so that he almost missed Sir Nicholas's next remark.

'Antony understands me well enough, and I think he should explain the matter to you.' He eyed his nephew with disfavour for a moment and became – as Antony later expressed it to Jenny – cross-examining counsel under their very eyes. 'Postulate for a moment that your client is innocent, as you seem so anxious for us to believe. What follows?'

'That someone else is guilty, I suppose.'

'And what else? Your client is charged with giving information, isn't he? What about the person who received it? If you think the other side, whoever they are – '

'Apparently, the Russians.'

'Well, if you think they're going to stand still while you quietly take an interest in their affairs – ' He didn't attempt to finish the sentence.

Maitland didn't reply immediately. Instead, he walked to the window and stood looking out, his instinct, as always, to take refuge in movement. Sir Nicholas was putting into words something he had known very well from the first moment of his agreement with Clare. 'I don't think that, of course,' he said, coming back to the fire again and this time throwing himself down in the chair across the hearth from his uncle's. 'The trouble is, I don't see what else I can do.'

'Because the request came from Clare?'

'Because she tells me Charlton is innocent, and Clare being Clare I feel bound to give him at least the benefit of the doubt. Heaven and earth!' he added, suddenly vehement, 'do you think I wanted to take it on?'

'I will give you credit for being genuinely reluctant – '

'Well, look at it another way, Uncle Nick. If Clare is wrong, don't you think one of us ought to keep an eye on her?'

'That could have been done without involving yourself. Mark my words,' said Sir Nicholas, apparently despairing of getting his meaning across, 'no good will come of it.'

At which Antony grinned at Vera and said, 'The gypsy's warning,' with less respect than he should perhaps have shown for the opinion of so eminent a counsel as his uncle. And was saved from any immediate riposte by Jenny's return with a tray containing four hot plates and a still hotter Shepherd's Pie.

IV

But if Sir Nicholas really thought he had pulled the wool over her eyes, he was the more deceived. 'He isn't pleased with you, Antony,' said Jenny, much later, when they were alone together and Antony had just succeeded in coaxing the remains of the fire into a blaze. 'What did he say to you while I was getting dinner?'

'He was merely pointing out the error of my ways.' Maitland laid down the poker and went to sit beside her on the sofa. 'Well, it isn't a matter I'd have chosen to interfere in, love, but I honestly do think Clare's opinion of my client is a good one.'

'I'd agree about that, only – '

'Don't you start lecturing me too.'

'I was going to say, if only she wasn't in love with him.'

He thought about that for a moment, and the look he gave her was half rueful, half amused. 'That did occur to me,' he said, 'and then I told myself it didn't make any difference. Now you're making me think of it again.'

'I'm sure you should.'

'All right, Jenny, I will keep it in mind. But you do see, if there's the least doubt about his guilt – '

'This,' said Jenny, 'is where we came in.'

'I know, but – '

'I'm not trying to be obstructive. Really, Antony! Only I don't think you should put your trust in Harry Charlton quite blindly, that's all.'

Jenny had brown-gold hair, an oval face, a short, straight nose, and rather wide-set grey eyes. She was a better listener than a talker, but her husband had learned by experience that when she did speak it paid to listen to what she had to say. So now he said only, 'I'll remember, love,' and meant it.

'And I did hope we could have one evening without Uncle Nick finding anything to carry on about, to let Vera get used to things, you know. I mean, it's all right when it's just us, we're used to him, or ought to be by this time.'

'I don't think you need worry about Vera.' Antony sounded thoughtful. 'Do you realise that our new aunt is quite capable not only of finding her husband amusing, but of letting him see it?'

'I did wonder once or twice.'

'There's no doubt about it. Or that he, in turn, finds some pleasure in her amusement. She may be the best thing that's ever happened to this household, Jenny . . . since you joined it, that is.'

'I'm glad you feel that, Antony, because all this summer I've been worried – '

'Not you too.'

'No, I mean I knew you were worried and that worried me,' said Jenny, making a great effort to express her thought clearly. 'I think you're wrong – '

'What are we talking about, love?'

'About whether we should offer to find somewhere else to

27

live. Don't tell me that hasn't been on your mind, Antony, because I shouldn't believe you.'

'You don't think we should?'

'Certainly not ask them, because it's obvious what they'd say.'

'You could tell a lot by the way they said it.'

Jenny disregarded this, intent on following her own train of thought. 'As for making our own decision . . . *I* think Vera is perfectly happy to have us here, and Uncle Nick would miss you frightfully. It's something you'll have to make up your own mind about, I'm afraid.'

'I see.' He was silent for a moment, and then he smiled. 'It's dreadful to think that Uncle Nick might become frustrated for lack of a sparring partner.'

'That's just what I mean. And you know you don't want to go, Antony, any more than I do.'

'All the same . . . oh, well, I'll think about it, love.'

'And as for Vera, it might even be a help, having us here. It will be a great change for her.'

'And a good thing too. I can't believe she ever really enjoyed the practice of law, whenever she got a really interesting case it used to worry her so.'

And *you* don't worry, thought Jenny, smiling at him. But wisely, perhaps, she did not speak her thought aloud.

THURSDAY, 14th OCTOBER

I

After a certain amount of telephoning on Wednesday, it had been arranged that Mr Bellerby should bring his client to chambers at eleven o'clock on Thursday morning. Maitland was on the whole relieved that his uncle would be engaged in court. Sir Nicholas had shown some signs of wanting to be present at the conference, while Antony wanted nothing so much as to be able to weigh up Harry Charlton without the distraction of the older man's presence.

Perhaps it was fortunate that Mr Bellerby was Charlton's solicitor. He was an easy-going man, and if he was – or so Maitland thought – rather more credulous than befitted a member of his profession, that had never seemed to affect his practice in the slightest. Now he was pleased at getting his own way and Maitland's services, and was beaming as he ushered his client into the room. Antony pushed aside the papers he had been working on and prepared to meet affability with affability, hoping as he did so that the fierce dislike he still felt for the whole affair was not apparent in his manner.

And, of course, Harry Charlton confounded all his expectations. Maitland, who had been expecting Adonis (perhaps as a fitting mate for Clare), saw instead a rather stockily built young man, very dark of hair and complexion, with mild brown eyes behind a formidable pair of dark-rimmed glasses. He came in with an alert air, taking in his surroundings (the rather narrow room with the inadequate window, so that the electric light was needed even at this hour on a sunny day), taking in the appearance of the man behind the desk, and obviously itching to get to the business at hand. At least, that was Antony's first impression.

Charlton waited until the introductions had been made, the preliminary courtesies exchanged, and the three of them seated, before saying, but apparently without rancour, 'I understand you had some second thoughts about me.'

That wasn't an easy one to answer. He wasn't sure how far his client was in Clare's confidence. He said, 'Do you?' non-committally, and waited to see what was coming next.

'First you refused the brief,' said Charlton, looking from one of his companions to the other as though expecting an interruption. 'Then Sir Leonard talked to you, and still you said No. And then Mr Bellerby tells me you changed your mind. The thing is, why?'

'I don't think my reasons need concern us.' An echo, quite unconscious, of the tone his uncle might have used. 'The thing is,' he added, repeating Charlton's words, 'that so far I know next to nothing about this matter. I haven't even seen my brief.'

'That isn't surprising,' said Mr Bellerby cheerfully, 'since it hasn't yet been prepared.' He knew Maitland and his ways well enough to realise that no criticism was implied; well enough, too, to know that he was very unlikely to have read the brief at this stage of the proceedings, even if it had been delivered. 'The matter is a fairly simple one – '

'I'm glad you think so.' That was Charlton, coming forcefully back into the conversation. 'You know, Mr Maitland,' he went on, settling himself more comfortably in his chair as though preparing for a lengthy spell there, 'it's interesting to meet you after all this time. I've heard so much about you.'

Antony nearly said, 'From Clare?' but remembered in time that perhaps he wasn't supposed to know of the connection. He was both relieved and irritated when Charlton went on, 'I've been with the paper nearly six years now, so I've followed a lot of your cases as they've happened. And then, of course, I went to the files when Mr Bellerby told me – '

If there was one thing Maitland didn't take kindly to, it was being reminded of the publicity that only too often had attended his affairs. He said, with a deliberate attempt at an emotionless tone, which wasn't as it happened too successful, 'If you will forgive my saying so, newspaper reports aren't always the best source of facts.'

'Don't you think so? Well, they gave me one fact . . . you can tell me whether it's true or not. Did your father once work for the *Courier*?'

'He did.' (And that's beside the point too.) He hadn't meant to add anything to that, but Harry Charlton was looking at him hopefully. 'He was one of their foreign correspondents,' Maitland said, as though unwillingly.

If the fact that he disliked answering questions was apparent, his new client chose to ignore it. 'He died ages ago, before the war,' he said, as intent on the story he was trying to extract as a terrier at a rat-hole. 'There was something queer about it, wasn't there? I can't quite remember – '

'Heaven and earth!' Maitland's patience was not inexhaustible. 'I'm beginning to see how you got yourself into trouble,' he added, grimly. 'All these questions!'

He didn't find it at all disarming that Harry Charlton looked surprised and a little hurt. 'It's my job,' he said simply.

'Well, this isn't the time to exercise your talents.'

'It's interesting.'

'Not to me. Let me remind you, Mr Charlton, that it's your affairs that are on the agenda at the moment, not mine.'

'We really mustn't waste Mr Maitland's time,' said Mr Bellerby, who had been listening to this exchange with some amusement, but now judged it was time to intervene.

Charlton looked at him reproachfully. 'I don't consider an exchange of information a waste of time . . . ever,' he said. Antony pounced on the admission.

'That's just what we want, after all. Take it I know nothing of what's been happening to you, and tell me – '

'Oh, that!'

'Yes, *that*. Have you the faintest idea – ?' He glanced despairingly at the solicitor. 'Tell him!' he commanded.

Mr Bellerby seemed willing enough to obey. Perhaps he felt that in the interests of peace it was time his client was suppressed. 'You put yourself in the wrong when you tried to obtain classified information,' he said. 'The penalty for communicating such information to the agent of a foreign state might well be life imprisonment.'

If they had hoped to impress Harry Charlton they were disappointed. 'I didn't communicate anything, so we needn't worry about that,' he said. 'As for the other, I'm a reporter, aren't I? It's my job to collect information.'

'Not when it's classified Top Secret,' said Mr Bellerby, with rather more firmness than he usually displayed towards his clients.

'I take it then' – this seemed to Maitland as good a cue as any to get back to the point of the meeting – 'that you deliberately went after this information . . . whatever it was.'

'Well, I'll tell you. There was obviously something going on at the Fenton Laboratory – '

'How did you know that?'

'I got a tip from one of the old stagers, Jack Bressler. He worked fifty years for the paper and retired three years ago. He'd always been helpful to me, I was pretty raw at the beginning, you know, and before he left he told me to keep an eye on what Basil Vlasov was doing, because there'd be a story there one day.'

Maitland, who had produced an old envelope from his pocket and was making what appeared to be some indecipherable notes on the back, looked up sharply at that. 'Wait a bit!' he said. 'Did you say Basil Vlasov?'

'I did. Why, do you know him?'

In the circumstances, this further question must be deemed forgivable. 'I knew him briefly, thirteen or fourteen years ago. He was Chief of Research at a firm in Yorkshire, that's why we lost touch, I expect, his being so far away.' He paused, realising that this was not the exact truth, and letting his mind wander for a moment to Mardingley, and the cold winter days on the moor. Did this make things easier, or more difficult? 'I was pretty raw myself then,' he said, and for the first time smiled at his client.

Harry Charlton returned the smile with an appearance of caution. 'What Jack said was that Vlasov was a brilliant man. He had this idea . . . I suppose it's all right to talk to you about it?'

'If it's as secret as all that the case will probably be heard in camera. But, yes, it will be quite in order to tell us about it. At the moment, however, I'd rather hear exactly what happened.'

'If you think a newspaperman can give you a straight story. You didn't seem to have much opinion of our accuracy, a moment ago.'

Maitland laughed. He seemed to have relaxed a little. 'I'm afraid that's true,' he agreed. 'But in the circumstances I'm sure I can trust you to do your best.'

To his relief, Charlton showed no sign of taking offence. Instead he remarked inconsequently (but obviously it was the nicest thing he could find to say), 'Clare thinks the world of you. Clare Canning,' he added, when Antony did not immediately respond.

'Clare . . . yes, I see.'

'She isn't a child any longer, you know. In fact . . . well, never mind that. She told me all about the trial, when she had to give evidence, but I expect there are a few things she didn't know.'

If questioning was his normal mode of conversation, as seemed to be the case, no doubt he had by now a fair grasp of the subject. 'You had got as far as telling us that Basil Vlasov had an idea,' said Maitland encouragingly.

'If you know him, you can tell me what he's like.'

'Your friend said, brilliant. Let's leave it at that for the moment.'

'But, I hardly – '

'You're interested. I know.' He did not stop to think that might not have been what Charlton was going to say. 'But the purpose of this meeting is to inform me of the state of affairs. I'm sure Mr Bellerby explained that to you.'

'There isn't really much to tell,' said Charlton, resigning

B

himself. 'The Fenton Laboratory is in South Ealing . . . well, nearer Gunnersbury Park, really. I began to hang around a pub there, the Mariners' Arms; and why it should be called that so far inland, I haven't the faintest idea. Anyway, when I had a bit of free time I used to go there. Occasionally, you know, it was a long-term project, and gradually I got to know some of the chaps who used the pub, including a group from the lab.'

'You started this . . . project, you called it, didn't you? You started it three years ago.'

'Yes, soon after Jack retired. He was a wise old bird, really, and his tips usually paid off. Well, about six months ago I couldn't help noticing an air of suppressed excitement about them – my friends from the lab – and that made me curious, of course.'

'Of course,' agreed Maitland gravely. If it weren't for the chap's confounded habit of asking questions, he would be finding his client rather good value; not least because of the refreshingly casual way in which he treated what was a very serious charge. 'You're going to tell me that you made it your business to find out what this air of suppressed excitement was about.'

'Well, of course I wanted to know. It's what it's all about, after all.' He didn't wait for any assurance of understanding, perhaps he knew none would be forthcoming, but plunged straight on with his story. 'There was one chap in particular I thought might tell me what I wanted to know; he wasn't above dropping hints about a wonderful new breakthrough . . . things like that. So I took steps to separate him from the others, got him to meet me in town one evening. He didn't tell me anything that time, but a week later – '

'At that point, exactly what did you know of the project?'

'That it was classified Top Secret, and that it was being funded by a Government grant,' said Charlton promptly.

Maitland cast a despairing look in the solicitor's direction. 'You'd better tell me at this point just what Basil and his crew are up to.'

'It's rather complicated.'

'A broad outline will do. No technicalities.'

Harry Charlton closed his eyes and began to recite something he had obviously memorised. 'The scheme is for a very high-speed, long-range, ground-following missile system intended to be launched in flights controlled so as to fly in formation . . . do you follow me?'

'With difficulty.'

'I'm doing my best. The idea is that each formation will contain members whose only function is to jam the enemy's detection equipment, so that the missiles with live warheads are pretty well sure of getting through his defences. The code name is Ashur.'

'Why?'

'Jim Rickover told me that. He said it was a sort of joke Julian Shacklock had thought up . . . he's the Chief Electrical Engineer and was with Vlasov from the beginning. The Assyrians were called the children of Ashur – '

'How on earth did the Assyrians get into this?'

'Well, there's that famous poem that starts, *The Assyrian came down like the wolf on the fold*, so Julian thought – '

'Byron,' said Mr Bellerby, unexpectedly.

'Never mind that,' said Antony, beginning to regret that he had requested the information in the first place.

'Yes, but don't you think it's interesting?' enquired Charlton, hurt.

'Very likely, but what matters at the moment is that, as far as this part of the story is concerned, we haven't a leg to stand on,' said Maitland ruefully.

'It gets worse,' Mr Bellerby promised.

'I suppose you mean I was technically at fault in obtaining the information,' said Harry Charlton, looking from one of them to the other.

'I had hoped we had made that clear.'

'Well, I knew we couldn't use it at this stage, but forewarned is forearmed, and when the story broke – '

'And this was the only information you gained from your

friend: the code name of the project and roughly what the –
should I say missile or missiles? – what it was capable of?'

'That was all.'

'Did you commit anything to writing? If you wanted to
have a story ready – '

'I wasn't quite fool enough for that.'

'There is then something at least to be thankful for.'

'You do realise my position, don't you?' For the first time,
Charlton sounded a little anxious. 'I didn't pass the information on.'

'We understand that,' said Mr Bellerby, that advocate of
kindness to clients. Maitland threw him an exasperated look
and said only, abruptly:

'What happened next?'

'Nothing, as far as I was concerned, until two chaps came
asking questions.' Charlton's tone was still vaguely dissatisfied.
'Special Branch, they said they were. Then a day or two later
they charged me and Clare said . . . well, anyway, it seemed
a good idea to ask Mr Bellerby's help.'

Maitland glanced at the solicitor again. 'You'd better fill
in the blanks,' he suggested.

'It became known,' said Mr Bellerby, readily enough, but
then he paused. 'Don't ask me to explain that,' he went on.
'*I* don't know how these things are done.'

'I expect Mr Maitland could enlighten us. Couldn't you?'
asked Harry Charlton.

Antony gave him a look in which there was very little of
Christian charity. 'It isn't relevant for the moment,' he said.
And then, turning back to Mr Bellerby again, 'It became
known – ' he prompted.

'Yes, well, that the information had somehow got itself to
Russia,' said the solicitor, with less clarity than that with
which he usually expounded his cases.

'Just the information that Mr Charlton has admitted extract-
ing from his friend? The code name and the nature of the
project?'

'Just that and no more. So they started enquiries at the laboratory, you see – '

'And Jim had an attack of conscience and told them about our conversation,' said Charlton, interrupting without ceremony. 'That was the position when they first came to see me.'

'And then – '

'A man named Foster volunteered a statement.' That was Mr Bellerby again, speaking to what he knew. 'He said he had overheard a conversation between Mr Charlton and his friend at the Russian Embassy, Vladimir Solovki. You'll find the details in your brief, but as reported it was obviously an exchange of the vital information.'

'Wait a bit! Did this man Foster know Solovki?'

'He described him accurately enough. The nature of the conversation he overheard made him interested, he said.'

'Thank you. And so?'

'Mr Charlton denies that any such conversation took place, but Foster picked him out in an identification parade.'

'Where and when was the conversation supposed to be held?'

'At a restaurant called Jenners' – '

'I know it. In Blackhorse Street.'

'That's right.'

'Was Foster dining there, waiting at table? How did he come to overhear?'

'He was dining, he says. I don't think myself he could have heard anything,' Harry Charlton volunteered, and didn't seem either surprised or put out when Maitland turned on him with something like a snarl.

'Don't you think you might have chosen a less public place?'

'But I didn't tell Vladimir about Ashur, I told you that,' Charlton protested.

'Where was your conversation with Jim Rickover held?'

'At Jenners' too. I didn't think of anybody listening.'

'Come now, you're not such an innocent as that.'

'It will have occurred to you,' put in Mr Bellerby in something of a hurry, 'that one conversation might have been mistaken for the other. But Foster was quite clear that it was Mr Charlton who was imparting the information, and there is besides the fact that the description he gave of Mr Solovki could not by any stretch of the imagination be applied to Rickover.'

'That's a pity. But only,' he added, with a rather sour glance at his client, 'what we might have expected, I suppose.'

'Foster gave the date of the conversation exactly,' Mr Bellerby told him, 'which I, for one, find a suspicious circumstance after such a lapse of time.' From his tone you might have gathered that he didn't altogether expect to be believed. 'It was Friday, April twenty-third.'

'Of this year?'

'Yes, nearly six months ago.'

'Did he explain the delay in coming forward with his evidence?'

'He had been thinking it over and had come to the conclusion it was something the authorities should know.'

'Hang that for a tale.'

'You think something can be made of the point?'

'Something. Not enough.'

'And I can't provide you with an alibi,' said Charlton. To Antony's ears he seemed to be taking a perverse delight in the retailing of bad news. 'I think I probably was with Vladimir that night, Friday was one of the evenings we tended to get together. But it was just an ordinary evening. Look, he's an interesting chap, very good English, appreciates the theatre, and opera, and ballet of course, though he always says ours isn't up to theirs, you know. Plenty to talk about, anyway, without getting on to forbidden topics.'

'And Mr Solovki's evidence, naturally, is not available?'

'There was no question of anything, of course, except a voluntary statement, but he is said to have left the country.'

'Back to Russia?'

'Presumably.'

'Was that in the recent clearance?'

Both his companions seemed to have heard what had hap-

pened, which wasn't surprising. 'I don't think,' said Mr
Bellerby cautiously, 'that he was one of those asked to leave.'

'I see.' He thought about that for a moment until Charlton
burst in impulsively.

'That was when they arrested me. And I was in custody
until the Magistrates' Court hearing the next day. And while
I was gone they searched the flat.'

Something Clare hadn't told him. Something perhaps so
humiliating that to speak of it afterwards would have been too
painful. But his client wasn't here to be sympathised with.
Maitland said dryly, 'From your tone, Mr Charlton, I gather
the search was not altogether unsuccessful.'

'It depends what you mean . . . but that's the queer thing.
They found some pages of figures, some drawings, that they
say were to do with Ashur.'

Maitland's look became intent. 'Was this evidence adduced
in the Magistrates' Court?' he asked sharply.

'It was. You can imagine how it sounded.'

'I can indeed. Can you give me any explanation?'

This time Charlton contented himself with the one word,
'No.'

'And the police didn't oppose bail?'

Charlton glanced uncertainly at his solicitor. 'They made no
objection,' said Mr Bellerby.

'In what amount?'

'Five thousand pounds.' Charlton started to add something
to that, and then thought better of it.

'I see.' Maitland was thoughtful again. 'Is that all?' he
asked, looking from one of his companions to the other.

'Well . . . no.' The solicitor's cheerfulness seemed for once
to be somewhat abated. 'There is one other thing, but Mr
Charlton assures me – '

'Let's leave his assurances out of it for the time being,'
Maitland suggested.

'Very well. It is just that the sum of ten thousand pounds
was paid into his account at the Fleet Street Branch of Bram-
ley's Bank early in May.'

'Where did it come from?'

'That's just it, I don't know.' Harry Charlton took up the story. 'They looked up the paying-in slip, of course, but the signature was indecipherable.'

'You couldn't account for it, in fact.'

'No way. I've only my salary. It isn't bad, but it doesn't leave me with that kind of cash floating about.' There was the momentary hesitation again, that Antony didn't feel was characteristic, and then he added, with more than a touch of defiance in his tone, 'As a matter of fact, Clare suggested that she should say she'd advanced me the money, but I wasn't going to have her mixing herself up in this mess.'

That was the only sign of emotion he had shown so far, and Maitland, for his part, felt the first unwilling tug of sympathy. Perhaps it was this that lent a certain tartness to his tone. 'Is there any reason why she should appear to be mixed up in it?'

'No, of course not. Only . . . I don't know if you gathered from what I said that we're . . . rather close. In fact, we live together.'

'I see,' said Maitland, and sounded for once as if he meant it.

'No, I don't think you do quite.'

'Your personal life, Mr Charlton, is no affair of mine.'

'But you're a friend of Clare's. You and Mrs Maitland, she often talks of you. What I was going to say was that I begged her to go home when all this blew up. Only she wouldn't.'

Antony smiled at him. 'Perhaps she feels she is already at home,' he suggested, and was surprised to see Charlton flush. Change the subject then, to something likely to prove of less embarrassment to both of them. 'You haven't told me, you know, when you first noticed this unexplained sum of money in your account.'

'I didn't notice it. That's what flummoxed me so when they sprang it on me.'

'But surely – '

'Why should I? I know how much goes into the Current Account every month, and I live within my income. The ten

40

thousand quid went into my Deposit Account, and I'd never had any cause to ask for the balance.'

'And the documents that were found in your possession?'

'They were in a folder in the bottom drawer of my desk, the only one that locks. And if you mean, did I discover their presence before the Special Branch chaps did, the answer is "No".'

'Was there any sign that the drawer had been tampered with?'

'I misled you, I'm afraid. It locks, but I don't usually bother about that.'

'What do you normally keep in this unlocked drawer?'

'The lease of the apartment . . . insurance policies . . . things like that. I don't often have occasion to open it.'

'Then you have no idea how long the folder had been there?'

'No idea at all.' He paused, and then added deliberately, 'I've got a feeling you don't believe a word I say, Mr Maitland. Is that because of Clare?'

'On the contrary.' (Time for a little plain speaking?) 'The fact that Clare loves you enough to live with you is the best thing I know of you, Mr Charlton.'

'Well, yes, I suppose – '

Antony took pity on him. 'We needn't worry about that at the moment,' he said. 'Mr Bellerby tells me you will plead Not Guilty.'

'I thought that was what this meeting was all about,' said Harry Charlton, recovering his aplomb, and with it a degree of belligerence.

No need to answer that. 'I think I have now got a very fair idea of the main points that the prosecution can make against you,' said Maitland, and realised as he spoke that there was one point that hadn't been mentioned, that Charlton and probably even Mr Bellerby, with his confounded optimism, had no idea of. 'If you have any explanation to offer that I can use – '

'I thought you understood. I didn't talk to Vladimir about anything that mattered, so this man Foster couldn't have overheard us. I don't know anything about the folder, and I don't know anything about the money. That's all there is to it.'

Maitland sighed and glanced at the solicitor again, from whom this time he got a look that expressed very well a certain fellow feeling. 'I'm sure you've got all the necessary enquiries in hand already,' said Antony. And turned back to his client and set himself, without more ado, to explain to him the difficulties of mounting a defence based solely upon his denials.

II

'But I don't know that he listened to me,' he told Jenny, when he got home that evening.

'Is he stupid?' asked Jenny, frowning over the thought.

'Not at all. Not unimaginative either, as far as I could tell.'

'Then I don't understand.'

He had put his sherry in its usual place by the clock, but now he reclaimed the glass and went to sit on the sofa beside her. 'His attitude amused me at first,' he said soberly. 'Only then I realised . . . Clare sold me a bill of goods about him, love, and now she seems to have done the same thing to him about me.'

'You mean, he's relying on you. Well, that's reasonable enough,' said Jenny. And then, looking at him a little more closely, 'That worries you, doesn't it?'

'It didn't, but now it does,' said Antony, with rather less than his usual lucidity. 'There isn't a single, solitary thing I can do about it, and the worst of it is I've got this damnable feeling – nothing to do with what Clare told me now – that he really is Not Guilty.'

'Is the evidence so very strong?'

'Cast iron. And there's another thing that neither Charlton nor Bellerby seems to have thought about yet . . . I don't see how we're going to keep Clare out of it.'

Jenny's eyes were anxious. 'I don't understand,' she said again.

'Well, first I have to tell you something that I don't think you'll like, love. They're living together.'

'Clare and Harry Charlton?'

In the circumstances the query, obvious though the answer was, didn't annoy him. 'Clare told me about it the other night,' he said, and smiled reminiscently, though not with much amusement. 'And we weren't to blame Harry, even though he's so much older, because it was her decision.'

'Oh, dear!' Jenny contemplated the situation for a moment in silence. 'I know a lot of people don't believe in marriage nowadays,' she went on, 'but I can't help feeling it would be so much more comfortable . . . or does it mean Clare doesn't care enough?'

'According to her caring or not caring doesn't come into it. And I'm afraid, I'm very much afraid, Jenny, she's going to get hurt.'

'Yes,' said Jenny. She still sounded thoughtful. 'Is that what you meant when you said she couldn't be kept out of it?'

'Not exactly. It will make the motive so much more comprehensible, that's all. Charlton has nothing but his salary, Clare has money of her own. Anyone would understand that he didn't want to depend on her for the luxuries of life.'

'I see what you mean. You think the prosecution will try to get that across?'

'I think they'll have a damned good try.'

'Well, what are you going to do?'

'About that? Do my best to get the evidence disallowed.'

'I really meant . . . in general.' She didn't meet his eyes now and he felt a sudden stab of anger; not at Jenny, who had never tried to hold him back from anything he felt he had to do, but at the damnable misfortune that had brought him into the affair.

'Bellerby's got Cobbold's working on the only possible lines,' he said. 'This man Foster's background . . . he's the chap who tells a very circumstantial story about overhearing the actual exchange of information. What do you bet he turns out to be a sea green incorruptible? Then there are enquiries at the restaurant to be made, but it sounds pretty hopeless to me. After that the Bank, it may be possible to get one of the cashiers to remember who paid in the money. And, of course, the question of who could have planted the papers in the apartment, and when it could have been done. I said I'd tackle that myself.'

'Because of Clare.' Jenny nodded her agreement.

'That's right. Charlton spoke at different times of a flat and an apartment, but I gather it's a studio at the bottom of somebody's garden, with the usual amenities tacked on. So I'm not very hopeful that any of the neighbours will have noticed anything.'

Jenny did not seem to have been listening very closely. 'I think what you're telling me, Antony, is that if Harry Charlton is innocent somebody framed him.'

'I'm afraid that's true, love.' He sounded apologetic.

'Do you really think that's likely?' She had stopped fiddling with her glass and was looking at him now, and in his turn Antony did not meet her eyes. Instead he got up, took a quick turn to the window and back, and was looking down at the fire when he answered her.

'I know it isn't a comfortable conclusion, but I explained to you – didn't I? – that, likely or not, I think it's true.'

'Of course I want you to help Clare,' said Jenny, and that was true enough. But she couldn't help adding, more cheerfully, as the thought occurred to her, 'All the same, I don't altogether see what you can do about it.'

He turned then and smiled at her. 'You and me both,' he agreed. 'I'll talk to Basil Vlasov too, but I don't see what good that will do.'

'It will be nice to see Basil again,' said Jenny. And allowed him, at last, to steer the talk into other channels.

SATURDAY, 16th OCTOBER

I

On Friday the brief arrived and was promptly concealed by its recipient at the bottom of a pile of other documents. It was true there were other matters more pressing, but it must be admitted that he was working on the principle 'out of sight, out of mind'. The more he thought about the situation, the less he liked it.

On Saturday, however, he had made up his mind to make a start at doing what he could. Have a look at the layout of the studio-apartment and some further talk with Clare and Harry in the morning, to begin with. A dinner invitation to Basil Vlasov for the evening had already been accepted. Though what good that would do . . .

In the event, however, his good intentions went for nothing. Before the first cup of coffee was poured Clare was on the telephone. She sounded panic-stricken, which was unlike her enough to be worrying. Antony held the receiver away from his ear, because her voice seemed to have gone up an octave or so, and waited until there was a pause. Then he said, in as bracing a tone as possible, 'Stop twittering, Clare. Take a deep breath and tell me again, quietly.'

'You weren't listening!' She was more despairing than accusatory.

'I couldn't. There are things of which the human ear is capable, and – ' He broke off when he heard her taking the deep breath he had recommended.

'Well, will you listen now? I'm quite calm, truly I am.' She took his assent for granted. 'The milkman found a man . . . dead. There are police all over the garden.'

45

If he didn't like the news, his voice gave no indication of that. 'Who is this man, and how did he die?'

'I don't know! Mr Maitland, it's nothing to do with us. But a policeman told us not to go out until the Chief Inspector could question us, so I'm sure there must be some suspicious circumstances.' She brought out the phrase cautiously, as though she thought it might explode in her face. 'And because they already think such dreadful things about Harry – '

'My dear girl, you're going much too fast. The man, who-ever he is, may have died of natural causes, or be a suicide. Even if . . . you're postulating a murder, but it's the wildest of guesses. And in any case, you've no reason to think that the police – '

'I don't think they need reasons,' said Clare stubbornly. 'You're sounding just like a lawyer, Mr Maitland.'

'That's why you called me, isn't it?'

'Because I thought . . . oh, please, will you come?'

'Mr Bellerby – '

'I knew you'd say that. He's out of town for the weekend.'

'Then I'll come. As a friend, Clare.'

'That's what we need.' There was a desolate sound to that. He was frowning as he replaced the receiver and went across to join Jenny at the breakfast table. He told her, briefly, what had happened as, still standing, he drank the coffee she had poured for him. 'Clare's having rather more than her share of troubles, don't you think?' he concluded.

'It seems . . . rather a coincidence,' said Jenny doubtfully. Antony put down his cup and bent to kiss her.

'Don't borrow trouble,' he advised.

He would have liked to take his time and walk, but for all he knew the matter might be too urgent for that. At the least, he ought to be there to calm Clare down. He wondered as he hailed a cab and gave the driver directions to the street in Bayswater that was the nearest he could get to the studio, how Harry Charlton was taking this new development. If only the fellow wasn't so damnably trusting . . . but there was also the question of how far he might be responsible for what had happened.

Find number forty-three, Clare had told him, and go down the little passage at the side between it and forty-two. We're called forty-three A, but from the street you wouldn't know we were there at all.

That, at least, was true. He made an act of faith and walked down the passage. Behind the house had been a narrow strip of garden, the better part of which was now covered by the studio. 'Matthew Holton built it,' Clare had said that too, reverently. He wasn't sure when Matthew Holton was extant, but the studio looked as if it had been built about a hundred years ago, probably planning permission was easier to get in those days, if it was necessary at all. A stone building, creeper-covered, with – as he discovered later – a hideous brick extension at the back.

What was left of the garden was, either by accident or design, mostly covered with a gloomy-looking shrubbery, with a flagged path winding through it to the studio door. There weren't quite so many policemen as Clare's description and his own lively imagination had led him to expect, and mostly they seemed to be standing around watching the short, tubby, white-haired man who was bending over the corpse. The doctor, probably. He didn't have time to study the tableau, a man in plain clothes detached himself from the group and came to intercept him. 'I'm afraid, sir . . . there's been some trouble, as you can see.'

'I only want to go to the studio. Miss Canning called me.'

'The young lady? Well, that makes a difference, of course. Are you her solicitor?'

'Does she need one?'

'As to that, sir – ' He let the sentence trail into silence, which was just what Antony would have done in his place.

'It would help if you told me just what has happened. And who you are, for that matter.'

'Detective Inspector Campbell. This is my manor. As to

what has happened, a man has been strangled, rather efficiently, with a necktie.'

'I see.'

'Did you say you are Miss Canning's solicitor, sir?'

'No. A friend, with some knowledge of legal matters. There seems no reason why I shouldn't be able to see her.'

'Well – ' said Campbell doubtfully.

'There seems no reason either why you should be detaining her,' said Maitland, carrying the battle into the enemy's camp.

'Until Central get here.' Campbell showed no sign of shifting his ground. 'Obviously, as the people most nearly on the spot, there are questions.'

'Obviously.' But there was something he wasn't being told, and it made him uneasy. 'I take it then you have no objection – '

He said that with confidence, but he was half expecting a rebuff, and was both surprised and relieved when the detective nodded briskly and turned to walk with him to the door. 'That's all right, sir,' he said, quite amiably now. 'The young lady will be glad to see you.'

He was right about that. Clare opened the door herself, and in a quite unaccustomed display of affection flung her arms round Antony's neck. 'I knew you'd come!'

'Of course you did.' With his left hand he did what he could to disengage himself; owing to a shoulder injury his right arm couldn't be raised very far. Not being able to use it, he began to feel as if he were being strangled himself, probably by an octopus. 'Now, look here, Clare,' he protested, 'things aren't as bad as all that.'

'That's what I've been telling her.' Harry Charlton, apparently as calm as ever, came to the rescue. Clare stood back, with more pink in her cheeks than was usual to her.

'Well, I'm glad to see you,' she said, as though otherwise he might have had some doubts on the subject.

Maitland smiled at her. 'Another time, let's take it for granted, shall we?' His eyes went past her to rest on Harry

48

Charlton's face. 'Meanwhile, you'd better tell me what all this is about.'

'Come and sit down,' Charlton invited. 'There isn't much to tell really.'

It was a big room. One end was clear of furniture, except for an easel with a canvas on it, a trestle table laden with what Antony mentally termed 'artists' paraphernalia', and a stool. There were other canvases stacked against the wall. The rest of the room was comfortably, if rather eccentrically furnished. Two divan beds, heaped with cushions; a sofa and a single armchair grouped near the fireplace; a small, highly-polished table with four chairs around it. Come to think of it, it was the colour scheme, and nothing else, that had made him use the word eccentric. There didn't seem to be any rhyme or reason to it; the only possible phrase was a trite one . . . a riot of colour. For some reason Antony's mind went back to Laura Canning's drawing-room, shades of grey with the merest hint of the most delicate pastels. Some reaction on her daughter's part? But there wasn't time for that now.

'Do you like our abode?' asked Charlton. For some reason the question came out jauntily. 'The bathroom's small, and the kitchen even smaller, but we manage to make ourselves comfortable.'

'So I see. But as we seem to be expecting a Chief Inspector from Scotland Yard,' Maitland said, hoping he sounded more casual than he felt, 'we'd better get down to cases before he arrives.'

'Sit down then,' said Charlton again. Clare had already taken possession of the armchair. Antony, who had never felt more like prowling, seated himself on the sofa, while Harry perched on the padded arm at the other end.

'The milkman comes at about half past seven,' he said. 'Clare was making tea, so when he started banging on the door I went to see what was up. He wanted to use the telephone.'

'Did he tell you why?'

'Of course he did. He said there was a man dead in the bushes, and I told him to go in and use the phone while I went to look. Clare wasn't dressed yet, but she was in her dressing-gown, quite decent.'

'And what did you find outside?'

'It was just as he had said. The dead man was smallish, neatly dressed.' He glanced uneasily at Clare, and Maitland said quickly:

'I'm not interested in the details of how he died. Just . . . had there been some attempt to hide him in the bushes, do you think?'

'That's what it looked like. As if he'd been dragged behind a clump of laurel, only in the dark the man who did it had left one foot quite clearly in view.'

'Did you recognise him?'

'It was no one I'd seen before.'

'There are a few questions arising out of what you've told me. For instance, why did you say "in the dark"?'

'I was out yesterday evening – ' But before he could get any further there was a knock, somehow a peremptory knock, on the door. Charlton broke off what he was saying, but made no move to answer it. Clare gave Antony a frightened look, as though she was asking permission to ignore it too.

'I expect that's the police,' he told her, back to his casual tone again. And when she still made no move went himself to pull the door open.

There were three men on the path outside, one more than he had expected. Two were very well known to him indeed, the third a stranger. 'Chief Inspector Conway and Sergeant Mayhew,' he said, and managed a welcoming tone, though to tell the truth he could have done without Conway's presence just then. And at the same moment that he spoke Conway, recoiling slightly at the sight of him and treading heavily on his companion's foot, exclaimed in a tone of deep displeasure:

'Mr Maitland!' And then, still more severely, 'What are you doing here?'

'Waiting for you to come in so that I can close the door again,' said Antony, maddeningly literal. Conway compressed his lips and strode across the threshold.

50

'Inspector Mayhew you know,' he said grudgingly. 'This' – indicating the stranger – 'is Inspector Wylie of the Special Branch. Mr Maitland, of whom you may have heard,' he added, completing the introduction.

They were all inside now. Antony shut the door. 'So you're Maitland,' said Wylie, in what Antony mentally catalogued as an ·'all is known' tone of voice, thereby earning his immediate, if illogical dislike. 'We came to see Mr Harry Charlton,' Wylie went on. He had obviously no intention of taking a back seat in any discussion that might take place, even if his more senior colleague initiated it. 'Don't you think you owe us an explanation of what you're doing here?'

Maitland considered that. 'I don't think I owe you anything,' he said then equably. 'But as you obviously won't be happy until you know I'll take pity on you. Miss Canning asked me to come.'

'You're also acting for Mr Charlton,' said Wylie. It sounded like an accusation. He was a smaller man than either of the men from Central, and he was as intent on his questions as a terrier at a rat-hole. As the thought came to him, Antony realised that he had used the simile before when dealing – or attempting to deal – with Harry Charlton's curiosity. But in this case it had an added aptness, Wylie wasn't unlike a fox terrier himself, thin of face and alert of manner, and his straight, rust-coloured hair did nothing to dispel the illusion.

'That,' said Maitland, 'is another matter, nothing to do with this. And, come to think of it,' he added, before Wylie could speak, 'I should like to know what *you* are doing here. Conway I can understand; Mayhew I can understand – I didn't know you'd been promoted, Inspector, congratulations – but why you?'

Wylie looked a little taken aback by this turning of the tables, and Chief Inspector Conway, disapproval in every line of him, took the opportunity of regaining control of the situation. 'We are here to see Mr Charlton,' he said. 'And a Miss Canning, I understand. Perhaps – '

'Well, you can see them, Chief Inspector. Here they are.'

He waved a hand, rather like a conjuror completing a successful trick, and the three men surged past him into the big room.

All this time, the two young people had been standing together near the fireplace. Thinking it over afterwards, Antony was surprised that Charlton had not taken the opportunity of inserting himself into the conversation before this, until he thought – and liked his client the better for it – that Harry was probably most concerned to allay Clare's panic.

So now he followed the three visitors further into the room, effected the introductions in as casual a manner as politeness allowed. 'I should like,' said Conway, obviously in no doubt of getting his own way, 'to see Mr Charlton alone.'

If that was a prelude to wanting to see Clare alone too, it had got to be stopped. 'I'm afraid that's easier said than done,' said Maitland, on a completely spurious note of regret. 'This is the only room,' he added.

'The kitchen – ' Conway suggested.

'Too small,' said Harry. Thank heaven for a client who didn't need everything explaining to him twice. 'It's no bigger than a cupboard really.'

'And certainly we can't send Miss Canning outside, with all that is going on there,' said Maitland firmly. 'So you see, Chief Inspector – '

'I see that you have every intention of using your usual obstructive tactics,' said Conway sourly. 'But I suppose there's no help for it.'

In fact, that was to take the reverse better than Antony expected, but he thought he knew why. To forestall the next move he said rather hurriedly, 'Miss Canning is quite willing to make a statement, but only in my presence.'

'You're representing her too?' said Wylie.

'I'm here as a friend. Miss Canning has no need of legal representation. If she had I should insist that she wait until her solicitor returns from a weekend in the country. And while we're about it, Inspector,' he added – his latest remarks had been divided between the three detectives, but this was addressed directly to the Special Branch man – 'there's the question of your presence here.'

'I don't understand you.'

'I think you do. When I introduced you I gathered that you knew Mr Charlton already, so I suppose you are familiar with his position.'

'There is no need to put it quite so delicately,' said Wylie, interrupting whatever it was Harry Charlton had been about to say. 'I know he has been charged with an offence under the Official Secrets Act, and that he is out on bail,' he added, and glanced at Clare to see how she took this very plain speaking.

'You ought to,' said Charlton. And then, to Maitland, 'He was there when I was arrested.'

'I see. So I think you must explain to me, Inspector Wylie, exactly what you are doing here now. Or perhaps Chief Inspector Conway would prefer – '

'There is no call to explain anything,' said Conway snappishly. 'You may take it there is a good reason for his presence, Mr Maitland.'

Inspector Mayhew, who had so far taken no part in the discussion, though Antony had been aware that he was taking in every detail of the room and its two original occupants, cleared his throat noisily. It was his custom to do this before speaking, rather like a grandfather clock nerving itself to strike. 'A very good reason,' he said. Maitland glanced at him sharply, wondering if it had been deliberately done to whet his curiosity, but there was no telling from the detective's rather bovine look. Mayhew was younger than his superior officer, shock-haired, tall, and heavily built. He had a naturally expressionless face that concealed very well a ready sense of the ridiculous.

'Then I think . . . I was going to suggest that we all sat down, gentlemen, but as you won't be staying – ' said Antony, and did not attempt to complete the sentence, except for a slight shrug that very well conveyed his meaning.

'Staying?' Conway took him up sharply. 'Of course we're staying. There are certain questions – '

'I'm sorry, Chief Inspector, but in the circumstances I really cannot recommend that either Miss Canning or Mr Charlton make any statement. I think you will find they will be guided by me.'

'Of course we will,' said Clare.

Charlton, who for a moment had a doubtful air, glanced at her briefly and then echoed, 'Of course.'

'You realise,' said Conway awfully – he was obviously simmering with ill-suppressed fury – 'that we shall draw our own conclusions from their refusal.'

'The only conclusion you can fairly draw is that I'm being obstructive,' Maitland pointed out. 'And I can't say that worries me particularly.' He paused, and then added, in a blatantly cajoling voice, 'Come now, Chief Inspector, it can't do any harm, can it? Just a few words of explanation – ' He stopped there, because it quite genuinely occurred to him that Conway might at any moment be carried off by an apoplexy. 'Come now,' he said again.

'It's a thing that can't matter one way or the other,' said Mayhew unexpectedly. Conway threw him a goaded look, as of one tried almost beyond his endurance. 'And since Mr Maitland is mixing himself up in the case,' Mayhew went on, 'he's bound to know sooner or later.'

Conway glanced, with uncharacteristic uncertainty, at the Special Branch man, and Wylie, who had been regarding his colleagues all this time with a certain amount of malicious pleasure, said cheerfully, 'Since there's no help for it, we may as well tell him.' And then, 'It's interesting to meet you, Mr Maitland. Seeing that you were once in the same line of business, after a fashion. I'll be glad to know what you make of the situation.'

'What s-situation?' Antony's temper wasn't proof against that kind of remark.

'No, this *is* interesting,' said Charlton suddenly. 'I didn't know – '

'What you don't know w-won't hurt you,' said Maitland

54

savagely. At the same moment Clare put her hand on Harry's arm. For one reason or another he subsided again.

'The local chaps got in touch with Central, and Central got in touch with me,' said Wylie. 'A watching brief, you might say, as was proper in the circumstances.'

'What circumstances?' asked Antony. It was touch and go whether his temper was lost again, but for the moment he was managing to hang on to it.

'There hasn't been a formal identification of the dead man as yet. Well, there hasn't been time. But from the contents of his pockets the local men had reason to suppose that his name is William Foster. And, of course, when we got here I was able to confirm it. Because William Foster, as I'm sure you know, Mr Maitland, is one of the witnesses for the prosecution in the case that is being brought against your client.'

Whatever he had been expecting, it hadn't been that. He heard Clare catch her breath, and a moment later she had left Harry Charlton's side and he felt her hand on his arm. When he looked down at her, her eyes were fixed on him imploringly, and he recognised unwillingly that he had assumed a responsibility for these two Babes in the Wood that wasn't going to be easy to discharge. Not that the description fitted Harry Charlton very well, he thought with a sudden, wry amusement; the journalist seemed still as self-possessed as ever, only his eyes followed Clare anxiously.

'It seems we can't reasonably object to Inspector Wylie's presence,' said Maitland, his tone making light of the implications. 'Could you bring up a couple more chairs, Harry, we may as well be comfortable.'

Of the three additional chairs that Charlton and Inspector Mayhew brought up from around the table, they each took one and Wylie commandeered the other. Antony sat on the sofa, and pulled Clare down beside him. Conway, after a brief hesitation, took the armchair, where he sat so straight-backed that he might just as well have had one of the less comfortable ones.

He waited, obviously chafing at the bit, until they were all

55

settled and then, after one inimical glance in Maitland's direction, proceeded to ignore him. 'Well, Mr Charlton?' he said.

Charlton took his time looking round the group as though for inspiration, but he did not, to Antony's relief, antagonise Conway any further by pretending ignorance of what was in his mind. 'There isn't much to tell,' he said. 'I came in at half past nine last night. There was nobody in the garden so far as I saw, certainly no body in the bushes.'

'It is normal procedure for you to conduct a search of the grounds, I suppose,' said Conway, on an inflection of sarcasm. Antony had his mouth open to intervene, until he saw that Charlton was quite capable of withstanding so open an attempt at intimidation.

'I didn't make a search, of course,' he said, 'on this occasion or on any other. But I saw the position of the body this morning, with one foot sticking out of the laurels, and when I asked him the milkman swore he hadn't touched anything. I have good night vision, I couldn't possibly have missed seeing him if he'd been there last night.'

'Were you with him, Miss Canning?' Conway turned to her unexpectedly. And Clare too, Maitland reflected, could surprise him.

'No, I wasn't,' she said, and as Harry's had done, her tone made light of the question.

'Where were you then?'

'Here, of course.' She tilted her chin. 'I live here,' she told him. Conway's expression became a shade more austere.

'What did you hear then, during the evening?'

'Nothing. I was working.' Her eyes flickered away from his for a moment, towards the easel at the end of the room.

'You were expecting Mr Charlton. Weren't you listening for his return?'

'I may have been, subconsciously. But I didn't hear anything,' she insisted.

'Not even when he did, at last, come in?'

'Not until I heard his key in the door.'

'When you say you were working – ?'

'Miss Canning paints,' said Charlton, forestalling her. 'And you can take it from me that she gets completely absorbed in what she's doing.'

'Thank you.' There was a touch of sarcasm about that too, to which Harry seemed impervious. 'What exactly were you working at, Miss Canning?' Conway asked. And again it was Charlton who answered.

'She's doing a portrait of me, but we'd had a sitting earlier in the day, she didn't need me again. She said it was . . . well, never mind that. It's on the easel if you want to look at it.'

'There is no need for that. We will turn to your own movements now, Mr Charlton. Why did you go out?'

'To have a quick one at the Dove and Pelican.'

'How far is that from here?'

'About ten minutes' walk.'

'You were on foot?'

'Yes. Why does this expedition interest you so much?'

'You must surely realise, Mr Charlton, that your movements last night are of some interest to the police.'

'Well, I don't mind telling you, but I didn't kill this fellow, you know, so it seems a waste of time.'

'If that is true – '

'Careful, Chief Inspector,' Maitland advised. Clare slipped a very cold hand into his, and he turned his head to give her a reassuring smile.

'I have been constrained to consent to your presence here, Mr Maitland,' Conway retorted, 'but if you are – '

'I know. By something very like blackmail,' said Antony. Oddly enough, his sympathy sounded genuine. 'For what it's worth, my advice to Mr Charlton is to tell you what you want to know.'

'I am obliged to you,' said Conway stiffly, which was only too obviously a lie. Then he turned back to his witness again. 'At what time did you go out?'

'After we'd had dinner, at about half past eight I should think.'

'Then, presuming that you took a direct route and did not linger on the way – '

'I didn't.'

' – you spent about forty minutes in the Dove and Pelican. Are you known there?'

'To the regular barman, yes. He wasn't on duty last night, it was a chap I'd never seen before.'

'Did you meet anybody you knew, then?'

'I had a conversation with a man who looked awfully like a bookmaker, and was probably nothing of the kind. He might remember me. But I doubt' – and now he was looking at Maitland, not any longer at the man who was interrogating him – 'whether he could tell you the precise moment I left the pub.' And Antony, who was liking the situation less and less as the moments went by, made no direct response to that except a slight movement of his hand, which might be taken as directing the witness's attention back to the detective again.

'I dare say not,' said Conway. 'Were you alone when you walked back here?'

'That isn't a very sensible question. I'd have told you, for my own sake, if I hadn't been.'

'Not necessarily. Not, for instance, if you had met William Foster, by accident or by arrangement, and asked him to return here with you.'

'Why on earth should I do a thing like that?' Even Conway, Maitland thought, should surely recognise the genuine bewilderment in Charlton's face. But the detective's next question made it only too clear that if he did recognise it he discounted it as a piece of play-acting.

'In an effort, perhaps, to persuade him to alter or modify his evidence.'

'Look here, if you're thinking of bribery, I don't have that kind of money.'

'The fact remains, Mr Charlton, that the garden here is one of the few places in this district where a murder could be committed without much fear of interruption, or of being observed. Were the curtains at that window drawn, Miss Canning?'

Clare gave Antony a frightened look and said hesitantly, 'Y-yes.'

Harry said impatiently. 'They're always drawn once it gets dark.'

'There's one other point you should be aware of,' said Wylie into the small silence that followed. 'Miss Canning is a wealthy young lady in her own right.'

'If you mean, she might have been induced to put up the money to bribe Foster,' said Maitland rather hurriedly, 'you have no grounds at all for such a suggestion.' But he knew, as well as the next man, that there were more ways of getting a point over to a jury . . .

Wylie's only answer to that was to shrug. Charlton said, as though he genuinely didn't see the point (which his counsel didn't believe), 'I don't see what Clare's money has to do with anything. You're saying I never meant to pay him, anyway, just to make the suggestion of payment as a bait to lure him here.'

'That's exactly – '

'You haven't warned us, Chief Inspector,' said Maitland, interrupting. Conway turned on him angrily.

'At this stage of the investigation – '

'I agree with you.' Maitland did not let him finish. 'But this stage of the investigation is also too early to be making assumptions.'

'Very well.' You couldn't, by any stretch of the imagination, construe that as a cordial agreement. 'Did *you* hear anything, Mr Charlton, after you came in?'

'Why should I have done, since you're assuming that Foster was already dead?'

'Harry,' said Maitland warningly.

'All right then. I didn't hear anything.'

'Did you go out again?'

'No.'

'You, Miss Canning?'

'I didn't go out again. Neither of us did. I made a hot drink and we went to bed early.'

This reminder of an irregular relationship wasn't calculated to please Conway, but his manner was so cold already that it could hardly grow any colder. Clare was obviously quite unconscious of having said the wrong thing. She seemed calmer now, but Antony wasn't under any illusion that this was easy for her . . . a nightmare from childhood suddenly made real again. He said, 'That's all very clear, don't you think, Chief Inspector? There can't be any need to bother Miss Canning and Mr Charlton any further this morning.'

'There is still the question of what happened earlier today.'

'Nothing happened.' That was Charlton, for the first time showing some signs of irritability, which might reasonably be put down to nerves. 'The milkman knocked on the door instead of just leaving the milk, and when I let him in he told me and asked to use the telephone. I left him doing that and went to look. Without touching anything, I suppose that's the next question.'

'Did you recognise the dead man?'

'No, I didn't. How could I? If he's Foster, as you say, I never saw him before in my life.'

'Not one evening at Jenners'?' asked Wylie. He had been silent for so long that his question obviously startled Charlton, who swung round to face him a little wildly. 'He must have been sitting close to you to overhear so much of your conversation.'

'Since his evidence was a fabrication from start to finish – '

'There's no need to argue the matter here and now,' said Maitland pacifically. 'In fact, the less said about it the better, until we get into court.'

'Then there only remains to ask Miss Canning whether she recognises the man.'

'I haven't seen him.' There was the note of something near hysteria, and Antony could feel her beginning to tremble.

'That can be remedied,' said Conway, coming to his feet.

'I told them – ' And at his words Antony too was shaken out of the calm he had tried so hard to preserve.

'If you think I'm going to allow anything of the sort,' he began hotly, and pulled himself up on the edge of indiscretion. 'When photographs have been prepared,' he said, 'they can be shown to Miss Canning. If you really think it's necessary to put her through such an ordeal.'

'A matter of routine,' said Conway smoothly. Maitland could hear the satisfaction in his voice, and knew, with annoyance, that it was due solely to his own momentary loss of composure. 'However, if you feel it would be unsuitable to ask her to view the body – '

'I do.' His hand tightened on Clare's for a moment, and then he released her and got to his feet. 'On the whole I think you've outstayed your welcome, Chief Inspector.'

Mayhew and Wylie got up too, the former giving his warning cough and saying, apologetically, 'There's just the little matter of the tie.'

'I hadn't forgotten.' Conway stooped to pick up the brief-case that had been leaning beside his chair. What he produced made Antony's eyes widen a little . . . a plastic bag containing a gold-coloured necktie with a distinctive pattern, a tracery of leaves in golden brown. 'The murder weapon,' said Conway with unmistakable relish. 'I must ask you, Mr Charlton – '

'If you're trying to say it's Harry's,' said Clare distinctly, 'I can tell you right away it isn't. I buy all his ties, and I never saw that one before.'

II

Maitland waited until the door was closed and he was quite sure the three visitors were well down the path before turning a somewhat rueful look on Clare. 'You shouldn't have done that, you know.'

'Done what?' Clare was all wide-eyed innocence.

'Lied to the police. There must be a dozen people who can

identify that tie of Harry's, and I didn't want you mixing yourself up in all this.'

'Well, do you think I wanted her to say that? I couldn't stop her,' said Charlton, aggrieved. Antony smiled at him, but Clare gave him no time to answer.

'How did you know?' she demanded.

'My dear child, I know you well enough to be able to tell when you're lying.'

'I don't think I ever lied to you before.'

'No. I remember.' His tone was gentler now. 'But there is also the fact that Harry was wearing that tie when Bellerby brought him to chambers.'

'Well, *they* couldn't have known that,' said Clare. 'I don't suppose they'll even think about it again now that I've told the – '

'Don't count on it, that's all.' It was no use being exasperated, he wasn't going to get anywhere arguing with Clare, though he was relieved to see that, now that the police had left, she was much more like herself again. He turned instead to Charlton. 'I'm glad I was here, in a way,' he said. 'But I don't suppose I've done your image any good in the eyes of the police.'

'I don't quite understand that.' Charlton was restoring the hard chairs to their place round the dining-table. 'I admit I didn't exactly take to Chief Inspector Conway, or to that chap Wylie either, but – '

'It isn't Conway, but you heard what he said as he was leaving. "Chief Superintendent Briggs will be interested to know we've met again, Mr Maitland." ' The mimicry of both voice and manner was wickedly exact. 'Briggs, you see . . . well, we don't precisely hit it off. He doesn't trust me,' he added, with careful honesty, and was annoyed all over again when Charlton countered that – as might have been expected – with the one word:

'Why?'

'It's a long story.' It wasn't a subject he wished to discuss, and perhaps Charlton, for the first time, saw in his face that this was not the time for questions. In any case he said, without waiting for anything more:

'I don't think it matters . . . what this chap Briggs thinks of you, I mean.' Something was troubling him, but Antony didn't think it was the point they were discussing.

'Well, I think it was a very good thing you were here,' said Clare, with perhaps undue emphasis.

'I agree.' Charlton had finished with the chairs now, and came back to the fireside. This time it was he who pulled Clare down beside him on the sofa. 'If it hadn't been for what Conway called your obstructive tactics we shouldn't have got any answers to our questions at all.'

Maitland thought again that it was good to have a client who didn't need to have things explained to him. He had been standing all this time by the door, but now he came slowly across the room again. 'The question is,' he said, sitting down on the arm of the easy-chair, 'who could have taken one of your ties?'

'I suppose when you come to think of it,' said Charlton, 'all this was deliberately planned.' Apparently the idea had only just occurred to him.

'I think so. And that's another question, the one you're so fond of asking. Why?'

'I haven't the faintest idea. I say, Mr Maitland, what did Wylie mean: you'd once been in the same line of business?'

'Nothing that need worry you. I have been solely concerned with my professional activities for many years now.' (And if they may have led me into unorthodox paths, that's something else again.)

'Mr Maitland was in Military Intelligence during the war,' said Clare. (Now, how did she know that? 'Uncle Derek', of course, damn him.)

'That's a story I should like to hear. Was that where – ?' Charlton broke off as Clare nudged him violently. 'Well . . . the tie,' he said, taking what was after all a pretty outsize hint. 'I wore it when I came to see you, and for the rest of the day. So it must have been yesterday – '

63

'Did you have any visitors?'

'No. But we were both out in the morning, doing the shopping. And we had lunch before we came home.'

'Somebody could have seen you go, if they had the place under observation,' said Antony thoughtfully. 'Have you had any consciousness of anything like that?'

'No. Should I have had?'

'I think you should. And that's a thought.' A rather startled look had crept into his eyes, but he did not stop to explain. 'Or . . . where did you have lunch?'

'At Jenners'.'

'I should have thought you'd have had enough of the place by now.' It didn't make sense, nothing made sense, except Charlton's guilt; and for some reason – could it be Clare's presence, which was undoubtedly a distraction, her obviously perfect trust? – he couldn't quite bring himself to accept that. 'Look here, Harry,' he said abruptly, 'why should anyone have it in for you like this? Is there something you haven't told me?'

'Nothing . . . nothing.' He looked at Clare, and then back at Maitland again. 'It doesn't make sense to me either,' he admitted. 'I could quite understand it if neither of you believed me.'

'Harry!' That was Clare, sounding reproachful. And then she said, and for some reason the words came out with difficulty, 'As a matter of fact, I've been wondering if we shouldn't get married after all.'

Charlton got up at that with a rather jerky movement. 'Not on your life,' he said. 'Not until all this is over.'

'I do think that's rather inconsistent of you,' said Clare. 'You've been after me for months, wanting to make an honest woman of me.'

'The only thing that would make sense at the moment would be for you to go home. I've told you that before.'

'Well, I won't. This is home,' said Clare. She turned an appraising look on Maitland, but to his relief did not try to recruit him as an ally.

'You know I don't want you to go, but I think you ought to,' said Charlton, but seemed glad enough to shelve the subject when Maitland came to his feet.

'There'll be more questions,' he warned. 'Tomorrow, perhaps, when I've had time to think things out a bit. In the meantime, there's this portrait you mentioned. Can I see it?'

'I painted it for you,' said Clare. 'To show you . . . well, you know, Mr Maitland, you always seem to understand what I'm trying to say.' She had got up in her turn and was crossing the room as she spoke.

'That's more than *I* can say. If you ask me, it's more or less a caricature,' grumbled Charlton, following her. 'Come and have a look at it, Mr Maitland, and see if you don't agree with me.' Antony went obediently in his wake.

It wasn't a large canvas and the portrait was, he thought, unfinished. In other circumstances he would have been conscious how much Clare's mastery of technique had improved; as it was he was thinking that she hadn't lost any of her old skill at catching a likeness, at getting beneath the surface of her subject. Here was Harry Charlton, warts and all; if she was right . . .

The first thing he noticed was the angle of the head, an alertness, an enquiring look. Those damnable questions, thought Maitland, suddenly, and for the first time, amused by the journalist's single-minded pursuit of information. But that wasn't what Clare wanted him to see; she must have known it was obvious to anyone who ever spent five minutes in Harry's company. She had chosen to paint him without his glasses, which gave his face a strangely vulnerable look . . . the last word Antony would ever have chosen to describe his very self-possessed client. But she might have something at that. It was the eyes, however, that caught and held his attention while he sought, vainly at first, for a word to describe their expression. And then he got it . . . integrity. Now, was Clare painting what she really saw, or what she would like to see?

'Very nice,' he said, and turned to find two pairs of eyes fixed on him anxiously. 'You'd do well to study it yourself,

c

Harry,' he added, not trying now to hide his amusement. 'It might teach you a thing or two.'

'That wasn't what I meant at all,' said Clare. She had never minded his teasing her, but perhaps she wasn't quite certain how Harry would take it.

'No, of course not. I do see what you mean, Clare, don't worry.'

But he wondered as he left them a few minutes later whether the reassurance had been fairly earned.

III

Saturday luncheon was another tradition, when Antony and Jenny joined Sir Nicholas, and Mrs Stokes, the other half of his entourage, put forward her best efforts on their behalf. Today, with Vera as hostess, was another first, and it was unfortunate that Maitland was a little late for the pre-prandial get-together. Jenny, of course, had been explaining his tardiness, which of itself was enough to try Sir Nicholas's temper. She was not noted for her lucidity. So there they were, all three of them, as soon as Antony had made his apologies and been supplied with a drink, expecting an account of his morning's adventures.

He gave this over the meal, in the intervals of Gibbs's attendance. His uncle made no comment, which in itself was ominous, and he observed without pleasure a number of uneasy glances that passed between Jenny and Vera. It was the custom to take coffee in the study after lunch, but when Antony got to his feet to accompany the two women Sir Nicholas stopped him with a gesture. 'Mr Maitland and I will take our coffee in here, Gibbs,' he said. And then, turning to his wife, 'I am sure, my dear, that you and Jenny will be more comfortable in the study.' After they had taken this not very subtle hint and departed, he waited until the coffee was poured and Gibbs had left them again. Then, 'You have some theory to cover all these happenings?' he asked gently.

66

Antony had been waiting for the question. 'That the whole thing was a frame-up from start to finish,' he said promptly.

'That covers the facts, certainly, but do you think it is likely?' wondered his uncle.

'Not likely, I suppose,' Antony admitted, 'but I think it happened all the same.'

'Do you indeed? Can you also tell me why anybody should go to so much trouble to discredit this man Charlton?'

'I can't, of course. Unless he knows something.'

'If he does, what is to stop him from communicating it, to you or to the police?'

'There's that. I admit, I don't know, Uncle Nick, but there's Clare to consider, you know.'

'I am aware of the fact. But you will not help her by deceiving her as well as yourself as to Charlton's true nature.'

'I don't think I am deceived,' said Antony stubbornly. 'And you know as well as I do, that if there is the faintest chance that he's innocent – '

'You would wish to give him the benefit of the doubt. That is all very well in the general run of cases, Antony, but here you're not just risking making a fool of yourself.'

'It won't be the first time.'

'Nor, I suppose, the last,' agreed Sir Nicholas caustically. 'But you didn't let me finish. I was about to say that if, by any chance, you are right you will be coming up against forces a good deal more powerful – '

Antony smiled at him. 'If you mean "them",' he said, 'I can't believe "they" will be particularly interested in me.'

'If you would stick to the strict letter of your professional duties and not go meddling in the preparation of the defence in so many matters, I should agree with you. But you have something of a reputation, my dear boy – yes, I know you don't like the reminder, but it is a fact just the same. And that is what makes me uneasy.'

'I'm sorry about that, of course, Uncle Nick – '

'But you don't propose to do anything about it. Well, I can't say I expected anything else,' said Sir Nicholas thoughtfully, 'having no very great opinion of your good sense.'

'I can't let Clare down.' (That was fighting in the last ditch, and he knew it.)

'No, but I hoped I had conveyed to you that I don't feel your proposed activities will be in her own best interests.'

'Let's leave it there, Uncle Nick. I'm not going to change my mind.'

Sir Nicholas sighed and assumed an expression of almost saintly resignation. 'I must not, of course, attempt to influence you,' he said, with apparently no idea that he was being inconsistent. 'I wonder if you remember, Antony, a question I put to you when you were defending Guy Harland with more enthusiasm than discretion. He was accused of treason, if you recall.'

'Of course I do. But what – ?'

'I asked you what you would do if your client was acquitted, and then, after all, you found that he was guilty. I might ask you the same question now.'

'You know perfectly well – '

'You said you supposed you'd shoot him yourself,' said Sir Nicholas inexorably. 'I have always believed that you were more than half in earnest.'

'You needn't worry. I've no intention of shooting Charlton, whatever the outcome. No, really, sir, you can't think I'd be quite so daft.'

His uncle gave him a long look. 'Very well,' he said at last. It was difficult to tell whether the declaration reassured him or not. 'Before we adjourn this meeting, however, there are two other matters.'

'Two?' said Maitland, startled. His uncle smiled at him. It couldn't, by any stretch of the imagination, be construed as a friendly smile.

'There is the question of your wisdom in being discovered by the police closeted with their suspect this morning. Chief Inspector Conway – '

'Doesn't like me, I know that. But there's no real harm in

him, you know. And I couldn't have left those two to face him alone; all this has brought back memories to Clare, I don't like to think what will happen to her if Charlton has to face a charge of murder as well as the other one.'

'I understand that very well.'

'I thought you would. There is also the fact that I got quite a bit of useful information.'

'Which would presently have been made available to Bellerby, even without your intervention.'

'Only if Charlton is charged with killing Foster.'

Sir Nicholas waved aside the point as immaterial. 'Am I right in thinking, Antony, that since Forrester retired, Chief Superintendent Briggs has been Conway's superior officer?'

'They work together most frequently, yes.'

'And in this case – ?'

'Conway did mention Briggs,' said Maitland unwillingly. That had been one of the points on which he had not been altogether candid with his uncle.

'Yes, I thought there were one or two gaps in your narrative,' said Sir Nicholas, obviously only too well aware of this. He was still using the quiet tone that meant he was seriously annoyed. Antony was too used to his uncle's irascibility to be, as a general rule, unduly bothered by it, but now he found himself wondering . . . 'I must tell you,' the older man went on, 'that I think in the circumstances you should be very careful in your dealings with the police.'

'No, really, Uncle Nick, they can't object to my doing my job.'

'I seem to recall that there have been occasions in the past . . . but I see that I need not remind you. There remains the question of Clare. Am I right in thinking that she is living with your client?'

'Quite right.'

'Without having gone through the formality of a wedding ceremony?'

'I'm afraid not,' said Maitland, and waited for the heavens

to fall. But his uncle only said, still with that dangerous gentleness:

'May I ask if this arrangement has your blessing?'

'Of course not! I didn't know anything about it until she came to see me that evening. But she doesn't need anybody's blessing in this day and age.'

If there was one thing that Sir Nicholas disliked above all others it was not being kept fully informed of any matter that he considered his concern. 'If you had thought fit to mention this sooner it would have given me one further argument to put forward against your participation in this affair,' he said coldly. 'Since this client of yours is so lost to proper feeling as to take advantage of a girl so many years his junior – '

'Clare says it was her decision, not his. He wanted to marry her.'

'Wanted?' said Sir Nicholas, pouncing on the word as if it were an admission of some kind.

'Well, yes, you see . . . *now* Clare wants to marry him, and he's the unwilling party. He wants her to go home until all this is finished, one way or the other.'

'Does he indeed? Were there any more gaps in your story, I wonder, Antony?'

'I don't think so.' He sounded cautious, and Sir Nicholas underwent one of his sudden, inexplicable changes of mood.

'That is all very edifying, no doubt,' he said, and for the first time there was a note of genuine cordiality in his tone. 'But it does occur to me to wonder – and I think you should give some thought to this – whether Clare did not know perfectly well what she was doing when she changed her mind.'

IV

They had friends in to tea, Geoffrey Horton and his wife, Joan, who was also Mr Bellerby's daughter. In spite of this, they didn't seem to have heard anything of Antony's involvement with Harry Charlton's affairs, so there were no questions to

70

answer. He was glad enough in one way of a respite from the subject, though paradoxically he was aware of a feeling almost of betrayal because Roger and Meg Farrell, who would normally have been with them, were in the country. Of all the people who were closest to them, he could talk most freely to Roger.

So it wasn't until the Hortons had gone and Jenny was putting the finishing touches to the dinner-table in expectation of Basil Vlasov's arrival that Antony had the opportunity of telling her about his discussion with his uncle. 'I don't quite see what he meant by that,' she said, when he had reached Sir Nicholas's comments on Clare's proposal of marriage.

'It's clear enough, really, love. A wife can't be made to give evidence against her husband, and if Clare knows perfectly well that Harry Charlton is lying . . . it isn't a pretty thought.'

'It's a perfectly horrible thought. Clare of all people! She's . . . she's transparently honest,' said Jenny, producing the phrase as if she had invented it.

'Don't you think I've been telling myself that? She is also,' said Antony gloomily, 'in love. As Uncle Nick pointed out. You know, Jenny, he's really taken this matter to heart. He says I may do Clare more harm than good by helping Charlton, if I'm wrong about his being innocent.'

'That's one way of looking at it, I suppose.' Jenny sounded doubtful. 'He seemed all right when you'd finished your coffee and came back to the study.'

'A truce, that's all. He didn't want to worry you . . . and now I've told you everything, like the idiot I am.'

'You know I can bear anything except being kept out of things,' said Jenny. 'But you're worried, Antony, by more than Harry Charlton's affairs.'

'Well, yes, if you must have it. I haven't seen Uncle Nick cut up so rough about anything for years. You know how it is, love, when he's really angry he goes deadly quiet. And I don't quite understand the connection, but acquiring a new aunt seems to have made me feel young again.'

'Young . . . and insecure?' asked Jenny acutely. She paused

71

to rearrange the table silver, quite unnecessarily, and then came across to join him by the fire.

'Unable to cope with him, anyway. As if – I know it's nonsense – as if I were thirteen again and had come to live here for the first time, and was dead scared of saying or doing the wrong thing.'

'But, Antony, you know Uncle Nick now. And even then, I don't suppose that feeling lasted very long,' Jenny protested.

'Not very long,' he agreed. He gave her a smile in which there was very little of humour. And then, seeing her look, 'Don't *you* worry, love. It'll all be the same in a hundred years.'

In a way they both welcomed the shrilling of the house telephone, which Gibbs had been boycotting ever since it was installed for his convenience, so that now it was apt to startle them inordinately. Antony answered it, and then went downstairs to escort their guest on this his first visit to Kempenfeldt Square.

Time had dealt kindly with Basil Vlasov, though he was perhaps a little plumper; otherwise he might have been the same sad-eyed, soft-voiced young man Maitland had known fourteen years ago, and when Basil smiled at him sleepily the illusion was complete. 'We're upstairs, I'm afraid . . . two flights. Do you mind?' And that was a silly question when he remembered perfectly well that Vlasov had been able to keep pace with his longer stride even up the steepest hill, and wasn't likely to be daunted by a mere staircase.

Jenny was waiting in the upper hall. Basil bowed over her hand – that was an affectation he had acquired over the intervening years – and then stood back the better to observe her. 'I don't believe it,' he said, in his quiet way. 'You haven't changed at all.'

'That's just what I was thinking about you.' She led the way into the living-room. 'Come to the fire, it's chilly this evening. How long have you been living in London, Basil?'

'Almost six years now.'

'And you never came to see us.' But they all knew why that

72

was . . . the same reason that they had gradually allowed Basil, whom they both liked, to slip out of their lives. He had been a good friend, but the experiences they had shared in Mardingley were not among their favourite memories. All the same there was a queer little silence, until Antony broke it with an offer of refreshment.

When they were all supplied he came back to the fire again, put his glass down near the clock and leaned one shoulder against the mantel. Basil, who had taken Sir Nicholas's chair, said as though there had been no interruption, 'And even now you want something from me, don't you?' But there was no offence in the words, only his own rather wry brand of humour.

'I told you as much when I invited you,' said Antony seriously. 'And that isn't to say I'm not glad to see you.'

'We both are,' said Jenny warmly. Basil paused to smile at her in acknowledgement before he said:

'Questions on behalf of a client of yours, you told me. I rather got the impression that you had taken his affairs very much to heart.'

Somehow you never expected Basil to see what was under his nose, and somehow he always did. 'That's true,' Antony admitted. 'There's a young girl involved, who's in love with him, someone we've known since she was a child. But that will wait.'

'I don't think so.' Vlasov was quiet still, but quite firm. 'Questions first, while we enjoy this excellent sherry. That's something we never saw at Mrs Ambler's, isn't it? No, seriously,' he added, as Maitland hesitated. 'Wouldn't you like to get it over with?'

'I suppose I should. Though you must be sick of questions about Harry Charlton by now.'

'I can bear it. It also occurs to me, Antony, that if you are taking a hand in the affair I have perhaps more chance of getting to know exactly what has been going on at the lab than if it were left entirely to the police.'

Antony in his turn had a rather wry smile for that. 'I

73

shouldn't count on it, if I were you,' he recommended. 'The police think they know exactly what happened and seem likely to be able to prove it. But I'm forgetting . . . you don't know that murder has been added to our other troubles.'

Even Basil's relaxed pose wasn't altogether proof against that statement. For a moment his eyes widened, but he said only, 'Tell me all.'

'One of the witnesses, a man called William Foster, who is alleged to have overheard the incriminating conversation between my client and his Russian friend, was found dead this morning in the garden outside Harry Charlton's studio apartment. He had been strangled.'

Basil took a moment to assimilate that. He seemed to be on the point of asking a question (probably, thought Maitland ruefully, one I can't answer), but then thought better of it. 'I can see that adds to your difficulties,' he said instead, thoughtfully. 'What do you want me to tell you?'

'I'll go if you like,' Jenny offered, but Antony stopped her with a gesture.

'No need, love. We're not going to be talking secrets. Even if he were tempted to divulge anything, Basil knows me well enough to realise his technical matters would be Greek to me.' (And that was a foolish analogy, because I probably remember some classical Greek from my schooldays, but it will have to serve.) 'As for what you can tell me, Basil, how about starting with the set-up at the Fenton Laboratory.'

Vlasov said lazily, 'It's a long story. However, if I must. I dare say you knew, all those years ago, that I had a project in mind that I was very interested in being able to follow up. I did put it up to Josiah, and he was quite taken with the idea, but the directors thought it too revolutionary, they wouldn't buy it at any price. Getting Government funding isn't so easy unless you're already established, and it wasn't until I met this chap Richard Fenton at Farnborough Air Show one day and he said he would consider putting up the money that I was able even to consider setting up on my own. In a small way, of course, Fenton's resources weren't limitless. However,

I was able to attract a few really good brains – quality being preferable to quantity – and to equip a place that would be adequate for our eventual needs. For the first two years we took on anything that came our way, made a small name for ourselves as being reliable, and then I put my idea up to the Air Staff. That was a worrying time, I can tell you, but we did get the go-ahead at last.'

'If you hadn't – ?'

'There'd have been nothing for it but to pack it in. It *is* a good idea, Antony,' said Basil earnestly, allowing himself to be diverted for a moment from his narrative. 'And we've been working away at it ever since, and I wouldn't be surprised if in the next few months . . . but that's of no interest to you.'

'It isn't exactly relevant, but I wouldn't say it's of no interest. You must be pretty bucked by the way things are going.'

'That's putting it mildly.'

'This – this disclosure that has been made, how important is it really?'

Basil's expression clouded. 'I could cheerfully murder Jim Rickover,' he said.

'Is that the chap who – ?'

'Who talked out of turn. Though I suppose what's happening to him is bad enough, and I shouldn't feel bitter. He's lost his clearance, and his job of course, and there are charges pending. But the thing is, he insists he handed nothing material over . . . I mean, he doesn't exactly remember what he said besides the name and nature of the project, but he's quite sure he didn't hand over the figures and drawings that the Special Branch people showed me and said were found in Charlton's possession.'

'You were able to identify them as classified material, I suppose.'

'I'm afraid I was. They tell me – they seem very sure about it – that nothing like that has got to the other side. Could they be sure about a thing like that?'

'If they trust their own agents, yes. The thing is, Basil, Harry Charlton admits quite freely that he got the verbal information from – I keep forgetting the chap's name – Jim Rickover, but he denies absolutely that he ever saw the paperwork.'

'And you believe him?' Basil's voice held neither credulity nor disbelief.

'I shouldn't be acting for him otherwise.' But even as he spoke there came into his mind that familiar, disconcerting flicker of doubt. 'He also says he didn't pass on the information he got.'

'And now the witness is dead.' That again was said in a completely neutral tone. 'But you asked how important the disclosure of that information was. Potentially dangerous, if it put ideas into somebody's head, but not immediately so. I'd been turning the principle involved over in my head for years, even before we got the grant, and even so we've been four years at it already.' And suddenly he was leaning forward, all his affectations forgotten, and saying earnestly, 'That's why I've got to know, Antony. If Charlton and Rickover aren't responsible, someone else is. Someone in the lab. Someone who could hand over the detailed information as it becomes available. Don't you see?'

'I see all right. That's just the problem I wanted to discuss with you, only I didn't think I'd find it so easy. When I ask you to speak openly of people who may be your friends . . . you're taking a good deal on trust.'

'I can see the necessity. And I don't think – remembering Mardingley – that you'd make the request if there wasn't a good reason for it.'

'All my clients aren't innocent, you know.'

Basil smiled at that, again taking the meaning of what might be considered a rather obscure statement in his stride. 'In any case, Antony, even if there were the slightest doubt of Charlton's guilt, I'd still want your help in finding out – ' He broke off there, when Maitland began to laugh. 'What's so funny?' he asked, and relaxed again in his chair, picking up his glass and beginning to sip his sherry appreciatively.

'You're turning the tables on me . . . don't you think? I mean,

I asked you here to pick your brains – well, I was honest about that, wasn't I? – and now you're trying to enlist my help.' He glanced at Jenny, curled up in her favourite corner of the sofa, and saw an answering gleam in her eye.

'Uncle Nick would have a fit,' she agreed.

'I don't quite understand,' said Basil politely, looking from one of them to the other.

'No, of course you don't. And it isn't really funny,' he went on, remembering his former misgivings. 'My uncle, Sir Nicholas Harding, whom I think you have never met – '

'I've heard of him.'

'Yes, well, he doesn't approve of my mixing myself up in an affair like this.'

Basil took his time about answering that. 'I should be sorry to be the cause of any family dissension,' he said at last, placidly.

'What he doesn't know won't hurt him.' Antony retrieved his own glass from the mantelshelf, and went to sit in the chair opposite the one his guest was occupying. 'In any case, it's fair enough. I shan't be involving myself to any greater extent than I should anyway in the interests of my client. I can take your word for the importance of what you're doing, just as you've taken mine about Charlton's innocence. Unless I'm deceiving myself about that,' he added, suddenly uncertain.

'That doesn't matter. I said, if there's any doubt at all,' said Basil. 'And that being so, where do we go from here?'

'To a consideration of your staff. The ones who know all about the project. The ones who frequented the Mariners' Arms during the time Charlton was going there – '

'They were being positively haunted.'

'You *knew* about Charlton's activities?' (Now, why should I find that so surprising?)

'I did. God help me, I even thought it was funny. It was quite obvious what he was after, but I thought I could trust my chaps.'

'I see. Well, that's two groups of people. Where they overlap, that's where it becomes interesting.'

Basil was thoughtful again. 'I suppose the first thing I ought to make clear to you,' he said, 'is that knowledge of the project is on a strictly need-to-know basis. Therefore, there are no more than a handful of people who have the complete picture.' He paused, watching Antony hunting through his pockets for one of the tattered envelopes on which it was his custom to make notes. 'You'll need that,' he went on encouragingly, as Maitland produced one. 'I never can remember names the first time I hear them, can you?'

Antony could, as it happened, at least as long as he was concentrating at the time – having a good memory is one of the things on which a barrister's living depends – but he only gave a rather abstracted smile and said, 'Ready.' The notes when he made them would be largely illegible, even to himself, but somehow the very taking of them served to clear his mind.

'The first list then,' said Vlasov. 'Vincent Brewer, who is Chief of Guidance Systems, and also acts as my deputy; Geoffrey Stevenson, CECM . . . Chief of Electronic Countermeasures,' he added, seeing Maitland's enquiring look. 'Then there's Julian Shacklock, Chief Electrical Engineer; Sheila Edwards, Chief Mechanical Engineer . . . and don't say that's a funny job for a woman, she's very capable; and Louis Yeatman, who is our Chief Trials Engineer.'

'Wait a bit! Would Jim Rickover be on the need-to-know list?'

'He'd know the part he was working on, that's all.'

'And the papers that were shown to you as having been found in Charlton's possession . . . would the information they contained have been within the scope of his knowledge?'

'There's nothing for you there, I'm afraid. He'd certainly have known.'

'How many other people – ?'

'The remaining members of his group, Edmund Waverley and Doug Watson.'

'Did they attend the Mariners' Arms?'

'Not regularly, I'm sure of that.'

'Thank the lord for small mercies. I need only concern myself, then, with the five people you mentioned.'

'That's right. But there's a snag about reducing the list any further, Antony. Only three of them were among the group who frequented the pub in question, but all of them knew perfectly well about Charlton's interest in the project. If it was a matter of supplying a scapegoat, as you seem to be postulating – '

'Heaven and earth!' He got up again and took a short turn to the window and back. 'That leaves me with seven people who had the information that has so far been disclosed. Plus Jim Rickover, who might not have stopped at telling Charlton. It's impossible, Basil, utterly impossible.'

'I still think that your first idea was the best one,' Jenny put in, her voice very quiet after her husband's emotional tone. She had been absent from the conversation for so long that her sudden re-entry into it had quite a startling effect on Maitland, who looked at her rather wildly. 'Think about it, Antony,' she added persuasively. 'If someone wanted to frame Harry Charlton, surely it was someone who knew something about him personally. That leaves you with the three names that occur on both lists; and, I suppose, this Jim Somebody, who might have been in the best position of all . . . don't you think I'm right, Basil?'

He wasn't willing to follow her quite so far, but he did give the idea his cautious approval. 'It gives you a working hypothesis, Antony,' he pointed out.

Maitland fetched the decanter and made a round with it before he answered. Then he said, 'A starting point, at least. Thank you, love. Perhaps you ought to be conducting this investigation, not me.'

'I don't think that would be a good idea.' Jenny was in no doubt at all about that. Watching her for a moment before he turned back to Basil again, Antony was aware of a certain wry humour in the situation. For some reason, which he didn't trouble to delve into too deeply just then, he was confiding in her matters that normally he would have tried to keep from

79

her, and instead of becoming even more nervous because of his disclosures she was responding with her own special brand of serenity. But there was no time to puzzle over that now. He looked back at their guest again.

'The people who went regularly to the Mariners' Arms, Basil,' he said, and made the words a question.

'Vincent Brewer . . . it was he who first told me about Charlton striking up an acquaintance with them,' said Basil. 'And Julian Shacklock and Sheila Edwards. I'd have said, you know, that they were all of them above suspicion. They've been with me from the beginning.'

'Is there any one of your people you don't feel that way about?' asked Antony with genuine interest. But he thought he knew the answer already.

'Well . . . no,' Basil acknowledged. 'And that includes Jim Rickover, before he admitted . . . which shows, I suppose, how little my opinion is to be relied on.' He didn't seem to find the thought cheering. Well, Maitland had known it wasn't going to be easy.

'What can you tell me about them?' he asked, his tone carefully casual. Not that he thought Basil would be taken in by that.

'Academically, a great deal. But that isn't what you want, is it?'

'Not really. At the moment, anyway,' said Antony, and waited.

'Well,' said Vlasov again. 'There are the personnel files, of course.'

'Damn it, Basil, you must know something about them. Any scrap of background information – '

'All right.' He seemed to make up his mind. 'Of the three of them I know Vincent best. He's older than the other two, middle forties I'd say, and the only one I've done any social-ising with. He's married, lives quite near the lab – well, we all do – and his wife is quite a formidable personality in her own right.'

'What does she do?' asked Antony, and 'What is she like?'

80

asked Jenny, speaking almost in chorus. Basil, looking from one of them to the other, chose to tell his story his own way.

'Her name is Susan, an old-fashioned name, extremely inappropriate for the very modern kind of person she is. Not at all the "little woman" type that men of outstanding intellect are supposed to prefer.'

'If you could tell me what she is, not what she isn't,' Antony murmured. This time Vlasov decided to humour him.

'She's Editor-in-Chief of a magazine called *The Weekend Review*.'

'A woman's magazine?'

'Not on your life, if you mean what I think you mean by that. The usual section on the arts, and so on, pretty highbrow; but mostly high-powered political commentary.'

'I'm beginning to see what you mean. But you haven't answered Jenny's question.'

'What is she like? Quite charming. And as far as I can tell – being a bachelor, I don't consider myself a particularly good judge of these things – as far as I can tell she and Vince were made for each other. In spite of their differences, or perhaps because of them, I've never seen a happier couple.'

'Their differences,' said Antony. It occurred to him that Basil had deliberately brought the conversation to this point. 'You say it's a political rag she edits. Is that what their differences are about . . . politics?'

'That's right. The description "pale pink intellectual" is far too tame for Susan.'

'I . . . see.'

'You may think you do,' retorted Basil, answering the tone rather than the words. 'It isn't Susan we're considering, after all, it's Vince. And he's just the opposite, a true blue Tory.'

'What a fascinating home life they must have. Do they air their differences often?'

'Only in the most good-humoured way. I think I've probably given you a completely false impression of them,' said Basil, thoroughly depressed now. 'I just wanted you to understand about Vince, that's all.'

'Your point is taken. It does occur to me, however . . . how about his clearance?'

'He was cleared at the highest level long before he met Susan; they've only been married three years or so. I don't deal with security myself, you know, and I've never heard there was any question raised when he came up for renewal. I expect the authorities consider, as I do, that Susan's bark is worse than her bite. You have to bear in mind the possibility that she exaggerates her opinions because that will be popular with a certain class of reader.'

'I see,' said Antony again. He caught Jenny's eye and, seeing her about to speak, shook his head at her. 'What about the others?' he asked.

'Julian isn't married. He's an odd mixture, I suppose. Utterly dedicated to his job, but likes a good time in his off moments.'

'What sort of a good time?' demanded Maitland annoyingly.

'All I can tell you is gossip, I'm afraid. As far as women are concerned he seems to believe there's safety in numbers.'

'His salary – ?'

'I'd have to go to the personnel files for that, too. If he were keeping an expensive mistress it might be different, but I imagine what he's paid is more than adequate for the kind of casual entertaining he goes in for. And he's an attractive chap, I didn't make that clear, did I? I should imagine he can find plenty of amusement without having to pay for special favours, you know.'

'How old is this attractive man-about-town?'

'Middle to late thirties. I'm sorry to be so vague.'

'It doesn't matter. You're giving me a very good picture. There remains the rose among the thorns . . . Sheila Edwards.'

Basil grinned at that. 'She wouldn't thank you for the description,' he said. 'A very down-to-earth person, our Sheila. She's married too, by the way, to the headmaster of one of the local comprehensive schools. They spend their weekends climbing, things like that. Anything that gets them away from the comforts of home. And I'd guess Sheila to be about the same age as Julian; I'm going really on the amount of experience she had before coming to us, I can't pretend to be any good at women's ages.'

'Do you know anything about the Edwardses' political persuasions?'

'Not a thing. Labour, I'd guess, but – '

'I forgot to ask you that question about Julian Shacklock.'

'I'm pretty sure he keeps himself too busy to bother about things like that.' Basil paused a moment, sipping his sherry. 'You aren't forgetting about Jim Rickover, are you?'

'I was coming to him.'

'After all, we know he spilled the beans to Charlton, and even allowing *his* innocence, there's nothing to have stopped Jim from having done it a second time.'

Maitland devoted a moment to admiring the rather schoolboyish turn of phrase. Then he said, slowly, 'I know it's possible, but somehow I don't think . . . not unless Charlton's guilty, after all. I'm thinking, you know, that somebody was in touch with the other side, not that the leak was more or less accidental, as it seems to have been in his case.'

'That's just why I find it easier to believe. If you knew these people, Antony – '

'I know, I know. Don't think I don't sympathise with your point of view. But you're not a political animal, Basil, any more than I am. You've just got to remember that someone who has been bitten by an ideological bug can become the equivalent of a religious fanatic, utterly dedicated. You used that phrase a moment ago – didn't you? – but it was to describe quite a different state of mind.'

Basil nodded his agreement, but he didn't look as if the explanation gave him any comfort at all. 'I'll tell you what little I know about Jim, anyway,' he said. 'He's in his late twenties – '

'About Charlton's age.'

' – and he's been with us for nearly four years. Good at his job, there'd have been a promotion for him soon if all this hadn't happened.'

'There's no snobbishness about this group at the pub, I

gather. The heads of departments don't mind hobnobbing with the rank and file.'

'That's quite true. All the same,' said Basil thoughtfully, 'now I come to think of it, Jim was a little young for the company he was keeping.'

'I'll bear it in mind.' It was only too obvious that Basil, having already faced the fact of Jim's betrayal, would rather consider him than any of the others for any further mischief-making there might have been. 'You were telling me about him,' Antony went on.

'A likeable chap . . . that's half the trouble, I suppose. Unmarried. I seem to have heard there's a girl, but whether they are engaged or not – '

'Never mind,' said Antony, as Basil stopped with a helpless gesture. 'I can't approach him directly, because he's one of the witnesses against Harry Charlton in the Official Secrets business, and that's still all the official connection I have with the case. But I'll be seeing the others, if you permit me, on Monday, and I may get a clearer picture of him from them.'

'You want to come out to the lab?'

'That seems the easiest course. Do you mind?'

'Of course not. And if I know you,' said Basil, draining his glass and eyeing Antony hopefully, 'you'll have thought up a whole list of new questions to ask me by that time.'

'I shouldn't wonder.' Antony came to his feet. 'Have we time for another round, Jenny, or is dinner spoiling?'

'Everything's under control. And I think Basil needs another, after all that talking. Can we forget about Harry Charlton for a little while now?'

'I'm all for it. And I'm grateful for your patience, Basil, but you were quite right. It's good to get all that behind us.'

It cannot be said of either Antony or Jenny that they did not spare a thought for Clare during the evening, but not even Basil, who was acute enough for all his apparent sleepiness, could have guessed it. When Antony saw him out at about eleven-thirty, he could congratulate himself that the reunion had been a success.

SUNDAY, 17th OCTOBER

I

It had been Maitland's intention to take a quiet day, spending perhaps an hour with Harry Charlton and Clare in the afternoon when he had some further questions for them. But in the event this peaceful resolve was frustrated by Clare, who arrived at about eleven o'clock, when the breakfast things had been washed up and they had settled down to enjoy the Sunday papers; in so far as anybody, these days, can be said to enjoy those heralds of doom.

Clare's visit was announced by a rather agitated call from Gibbs on the house phone to say that she was already on her way upstairs, and Antony had no sooner replaced the receiver than she erupted into the hall looking like nothing so much (as he told Jenny later) as a cat whose fur had been brushed up the wrong way. All this was so unlike her usual manner that for a moment he could only stare at her, while Clare, having swept the door shut behind her with a dramatic gesture said no more than, 'Mr Maitland!' and burst into tears.

For a few minutes after that everything was confusion. Jenny fortunately arrived on the scene, succeeded in persuading Clare into the living-room, and despatched Antony for a glass of water. When he returned with this Clare was seated on the sofa, still crying, but when Jenny told her to 'Drink this' she made a real effort to calm herself. The glass rattled against her teeth, but she drank some of the water, and then looked up and said, though still with a sob in her voice, 'He's gone!'

Jenny repossessed herself of the glass. 'Harry?' she asked. Clare nodded tragically. 'I'm sure he's doing what he thinks is best. Antony told me he thought you shouldn't be together just now, but when this is all over – '

'You don't understand. He wouldn't have done that without telling me. He's . . . just disappeared!'

Antony said, 'You'd better tell us.' And when she didn't immediately respond added more insistently, 'Did you have any more talk after I left you about parting for the time being?'

'Not another word. I did think of that at first, that's why I waited so long to tell you. But he wouldn't leave me all this time without a word.'

'No, I don't think he would.' If there had been one thing more than another that had impressed him when he saw them together, it had been Charlton's concern for Clare. 'Well then, when did you last see him?'

'He went out last night at about nine o'clock, just for a stroll he said, because he felt restless.'

'Wait a bit! Did he suggest that you accompany him?'

'He knew I wouldn't. I was still trying to get that portrait right.'

'I see.'

'He never came back.' She turned to look at Jenny again, as if confident of finding understanding there at least. 'I sat up all night, and then this morning . . . I told you that. When I couldn't bear it any longer I came here.'

'And quite right too.' That was Antony, trying to sound more cheerful than he felt.

Clare looked up at him and asked simply, 'Do you think he's dead?'

'Of course he isn't dead!' But it must have been doubt that sharpened his tone. 'Have you told the police?' he asked her, more gently.

'Mr Maitland, I couldn't. I know what they'd say. That the charges against him were true all the time, that he's defected. And I don't even know,' she added drearily, 'if that's what you're thinking.'

The obvious answer. It had been, of course, the first thing

86

in his mind. 'I think we must tell them all the same,' he said, avoiding what perhaps to her was the most important issue. 'If there's been an accident – '

Clare seized on the suggestion eagerly. 'Do you think it might be that? It would mean – ' But she broke off there, seeing the implications with sudden clarity. 'It would mean he was badly hurt,' she added after a moment, in a small voice. 'Otherwise he'd have made somebody get in touch with me.'

'It's no good despairing, Clare, until we know something more.'

'What are you going to do?'

'Tell the police what you've just told me. Only first' – he glanced at Jenny, thinking that she at least would take his meaning – 'I've got to talk to Uncle Nick. Will you two be all right?'

'I shall be making Clare some breakfast,' said Jenny positively, sounding quite unlike herself. 'And she isn't going to cry any more . . . are you?' she asked, with a reversion to her usual manner. 'Because, you know, it really doesn't do any good.'

'I'm quite calm now.' Somehow, with the sudden, rather touching assumption of dignity, Clare seemed a child again, which made neither of the others feel any better. 'Only . . . Mr Maitland . . . aren't *you* going to do anything?'

'Yes, of course.' No use telling her that for the moment at least his mind was a blank on the subject. 'Jenny love, even before you feed Clare, will you phone Basil? Ask him for the home addresses of the people we talked about yesterday. It's urgent, so if he doesn't know them offhand will he please take steps to find out? I'll check back with you after I've talked to Uncle Nick.' He paused only to give Clare a heartening grin, and was gone.

Downstairs it was very quiet, and for a wonder Gibbs wasn't hovering in the hall. The study door was open; he checked, just in case, but his uncle wasn't there. Disappointed, he was about to go upstairs again, when he noticed that the door of the big drawing-room was also standing ajar. Better check there too, though it didn't seem likely . . .

The room presented an unfamiliar appearance. To its normal furnishings had been added such pieces as Vera couldn't quite bear to part with from her former home; also her stereo equipment and her collection of records, which in its disarray looked even larger than it had in its previous place. Vera was standing in the middle of the room contemplating this scene of disorder, but she looked round thankfully when he appeared.

'Should never have brought anything from Chedcombe, Antony,' she greeted him. 'Can't think how to arrange all this stuff.'

Somehow it seemed to be important to answer her, without revealing at once the urgency of his own mood. 'It's going to be a music room,' he said. 'Arrange it that way, with the most comfortable chairs exactly the right distance from the speakers.'

'But that won't look right.'

'What does it matter? Look, Vera, Uncle Nick never used this room in the past except when he entertained.'

'How often – ?' There was definitely something a little wary in Vera's tone.

'About once a year, generally in the middle of the Hilary Term. When that happens we can push everything into some semblance of order, but in the meantime I assure you he'll appreciate the comfort as much as you will.'

'If you really think – ' It wasn't like Vera to speak in half-finished sentences, or to sound so doubtful. Antony, concealing his impatience, said:

'I really do.' And only then, when she looked to some degree reassured by this positive statement, added as though the query had only just occurred to him, 'Where's Uncle Nick?'

'Had to see Mr Halloran.' Vera must be taking her retirement seriously to use the prefix to his name when speaking of a fellow barrister. But he might have known she'd see

88

through his casual manner. Now she gave him one of her searching looks and said gruffly, 'Urgent, isn't it? Well, he shouldn't be long.'

'That's good. Look here, Vera, can I tell you – ?'

'Anything you like.'

'It's this business of Harry Charlton again. Now he's disappeared.'

'Know what Nicholas will say to that, don't you? Clear proof of guilt.'

'Do you think I don't know that? Do you think I haven't wondered myself? But even apart from my respect for Clare's judgment, which I quite realise won't weigh with you – '

'Perhaps not. Have considerable faith in *your* judgment, however,' said Vera, surprising him, so that for a moment he stared at her almost as though he didn't comprehend what she was saying.

'If that's true,' he said at last. 'Well, of course it is, or you wouldn't say it. What I mean is, I do believe Charlton somehow. And so I need Uncle Nick's help.'

'Tell me.'

'Clare was quite right . . . she's upstairs with Jenny, by the way, that's how I know that Charlton's gone. She said that if she'd reported his disappearance to the police they'd have taken it for granted he'd gone of his own volition. The same thing will apply if I try to get over to Conway that we really want him looking for. He'd set a manhunt in progress, which isn't quite the same thing.'

'See what you mean,' Vera nodded. 'So – '

'Uncle Nick knows the Assistant Commissioner at Scotland Yard slightly. I want him to persuade him . . . that Harry Charlton's guilt isn't a foregone conclusion, for instance.'

'Exactly what do you think has happened?'

'I'm afraid . . . desperately afraid he may be dead. There's just this hope, that a dead body is harder to conceal than a live one. But however it is, I think his disappearance has been contrived to create just the impression I'm trying to avoid, that he's guilty as charged, and also guilty of murdering one of the witnesses against him.'

'Enough to be going on with,' agreed Vera. 'More, isn't there?'

'Nothing that matters.' They had been standing all this time, and now he took a turn to the window and back, moving stiffly as he did when his shoulder was paining him.

Vera's eyes, following his movements, were sympathetic, but her voice was as gruff as ever when she spoke. 'Like you to tell me.'

'Uncle Nick could do so just as well. If Charlton is being framed, as I have to believe to have any faith in him at all, this latest move is probably made to clinch matters.'

'Obvious,' said Vera.

'Wait a bit! They might have left him for the courts to deal with if I hadn't taken a hand. As Uncle Nick would say, "my unfortunate reputation".' There was a tinge of bitterness about the mimicry, but it was none the less accurate for that.

'See what you mean. Don't need to tell you, Nicholas isn't always . . . mood can change, just like that.'

'No, you don't, though the change isn't always for the better.' He smiled at her suddenly, it seemed with real amusement. 'Can I leave you to talk to him, Vera? If I tell you just what Clare told me – ' But before he could complete the sentence, before he had time to judge from Vera's expression whether she would agree to his request, there came the sound of raised voices from the hall, a deep voice speaking in anger, and Gibbs's higher-pitched tone raised in expostulation.

'Better see what's up,' said Vera abruptly. But Antony had already gone. She followed him more slowly.

Later he realised that two men had entered the hall despite Gibbs's protests, but for the moment he was aware of only one of them, the one whose voice he thought he recognised, his old enemy, Detective Chief Superintendent Briggs. At any other time he would have said that word was too strong to describe their relationship, but for the moment it would do as well as any other.

The Chief Superintendent was a big man and had grown no less stout with the years. Even when they had first met he had had a high-domed forehead, now his reddish hair had thinned and was growing still further back until there was really no more than a fringe, back and sides. In general his cold blue eyes gave no hint of his choleric disposition, but at the moment he was angry, too angry for caution. As he caught sight of Antony he lunged past Gibbs and came to a halt no more than a yard from his quarry. 'All right, *Mister* Maitland,' he said – the courtesy title was given a savage emphasis – 'Where is he?'

Antony was well enough aware that his dislike for Briggs, which had persisted since their first meeting, was instinctive and therefore unreasonable, but this was too much for any good resolutions he might otherwise have formed. 'If you have s-something to ask m-me, you c-can do s-so in a reasonable m-manner,' he said. 'Otherwise, you c-can g-get out.'

It wasn't only to the detective that the slight, angry stammer betrayed him. Vera came up beside him quietly and laid a hand on his arm, an intimate gesture that was quite unlike anything she would normally have permitted herself. His anger died when he turned his head and saw her anxious look. 'I'm sorry, Vera,' he said, quietly enough. 'This is Chief Superintendent Briggs. Lady Harding, Chief Superintendent. If you really wish to see me, perhaps she will permit us to use my uncle's study.'

Vera acknowledged the introduction with a rather curt nod. 'Don't want to disturb Jenny,' she said. 'Use the study, of course.'

Briggs said, 'That is kind of you, madam.' It cost him an effort, but for the moment the hostility was banished from his voice. He would have denied that there was anything in the least irrational about his feelings: he distrusted Maitland, and his antagonism towards the younger man was therefore completely logical. If there were other causes for irritation, he wouldn't have admitted to being swayed by them. Maitland's casual air could be annoying, even more so the look of amusement that all too often crept into his eyes. Not that there was

91

much humour to be found in the present situation, the chap was glaring at him, even though he did seem to have got his temper under some sort of control. 'The matter is urgent, Mr Maitland,' Briggs added stiffly.

'Very well.' As he turned to cross the hall he saw for the first time who Briggs's companion was. Inspector Wylie of the Special Branch. It was something to do with the matter of Harry Charlton then; not that he had expected anything else. 'If you'll come this way, both of you.' It wasn't until they were all in the study and he was about to close the door that he realised that Vera was still among those present. He wouldn't have chosen to have her hear the sort of dog-fight that seemed likely to develop, but she might as well know the worst about him now as later. He shut the door carefully, and turned, and said, still carefully, 'Now, Chief Superintendent, what's all this about?'

'I think you know very well, Mr Maitland.'

'How can I, unless you tell me?' He was looking from one of the visitors to the other, and Wylie chose this moment to speak for the first time.

'Harry Charlton is missing,' he said. His voice was flat, completely without expression, and hearing it Briggs's temper was gone again.

'Not only that,' he snapped. 'He killed one of my men to get away.'

It was at this moment, before Antony had even begun to think how he should reply, that Sir Nicholas walked into the room.

II

He allowed himself a moment to take in the assembled group, then he said in his mildest tone, 'It is a pleasure to see you, of course, Chief Superintendent, but I hardly expected . . . and on a Sunday morning too.' His eyes came to rest meditatively on Maitland's face. 'Perhaps, Antony, you can explain.' But it was Vera who leaped into the breach.

'Burst into the house,' she said. 'Seem to think we're harbouring Harry Charlton.'

Briggs's wrath was still simmering, but he made a fair attempt to answer the allegation calmly. 'You misunderstood me, Lady Harding,' he told her. And then, to Sir Nicholas, 'The young man has certainly disappeared.'

Wylie said nothing, but Antony was becoming uncomfortably conscious of his steady regard.

'That hardly seems' – Sir Nicholas's voice was still gentle – 'to explain why you are here.' His eyes went past Briggs to rest on his companion. But Briggs was in no mood to consider such niceties as a formal introduction.

'One of my men is dead,' he said shortly.

'I am sorry to hear it.'

'Murdered by Charlton in making his getaway.'

'I don't know all the facts, of course,' said Maitland, 'but aren't you theorising ahead of your data?' He was trying his best to emulate his uncle's manner, but Briggs's obvious antagonism had shaken him and anyone who knew him well would have recognised the raggedness of his tone. Perhaps for this reason Sir Nicholas's next observation seemed to be addressed directly to his nephew.

'None of this really explains this – this incursion,' he said.

'*I* can't explain it, sir.'

'Perhaps if we could speak to Mr Maitland alone,' said Briggs. 'I have no wish to disturb you, or Lady Harding, but she gave her permission for us to use this room.' Briggs had recovered sufficiently to revert to his own more normal manner; dignified, perhaps, though Antony would have called it pompous.

'You feel he can help you?'

'I think he knows where Charlton is,' snapped Briggs, forgetting himself again. Sir Nicholas's eyebrows went up.

'What I told you in the first place,' Vera pointed out.

'So you did, my dear. Can you help the Chief Superintendent, Antony?'

'I know nothing of Charlton's whereabouts.'

'But you did know he was missing . . . before we told you,' said Wylie. (Was that something I said, or just a damned good guess? For the moment he was too confused to be sure.)

'Of course I did.' He turned to his uncle, ignoring for the moment Briggs's suspicious stare and Wylie's considering one. 'I came down to ask you, Uncle Nick, to phone the police for me. I knew if I did it myself they'd think . . . just what the Chief Superintendent's thinking now.'

'That you were responsible?'

'No, not that. Nothing so fantastic. That he'd gone because he was guilty, though. And I want an investigation into a possible kidnapping, not a manhunt.'

That was too much for Briggs. 'It has been obvious to me for years,' he said, 'that you would go to any lengths where your clients are concerned.'

'Just one moment.' Sir Nicholas's voice was dangerously quiet. 'You seem to be making an accusation of some sort. I should like it clarified. Of what do you suspect my nephew?'

'At best, of having engineered Charlton's disappearance. At worst, of knowing where he has gone.'

'Well, Antony?'

'You know the answer to that, Uncle Nick. Neither of those things is true.'

'I think you must tell me, however, how you knew that he was missing.'

'Because Clare came here half an hour ago in a state of great distress.' He was addressing himself directly to his uncle; the two detectives might not have been on the same planet, let alone in the same room. 'I thought at first Charlton had left her out of consideration for her, he was trying to persuade her yesterday to leave him. That may still be true, but I think he would have told her – '

'Yes, I think so too. What do you suggest as an alternative?'

'I think he was removed to ensure that no further enquiries

were made either into the leak of information from the Fenton Laboratory or into the murder of William Foster.'

'You do not consider the possibility – you must not think I necessarily disagree with you, I am asking for information only – you do not consider the possibility that he has gone of his own accord?'

'That would create a strong presumption of his guilt. I just don't believe it.'

Briggs, who had been simmering while this exchange was going on, broke in there. 'This is all very pretty, very ingenuous,' he said, sneering. 'You're forgetting the detective constable who was killed.' And when Antony made no attempt to reply to that he added the one thing that was necessary to complete Sir Nicholas's disenchantment with the scene. 'You may find it easy to pull the wool over your relatives' eyes, Mr Maitland, but I am not so easily deceived.'

The idea of Sir Nicholas being in the least degree credulous ought to have amused Antony. Instead, it sparked his temper again.

'You're accusing m-me, I think, of b-being an accessory b-before the f-fact to m-murder. You've h-heard my d-denial. What n-now?'

Unsatisfactory as Sir Nicholas may have felt this speech to be, it had at least the merit of bringing Briggs face to face with a fact he found unpleasant. There was, at this stage, no action that he could take. He said, blustering a little, 'As you say she is here, I should like to see Miss Canning.'

'Very w-well!' He half expected Sir Nicholas to intervene again, if only to rebuke his loss of temper, but his uncle seemed to have decided to leave him the floor. 'B-but first you'll tell m-me why you think a crime has b-been committed, what reason you have to think that Ch-Charlton has disappeared.'

'You have admitted – '

'I admit he d-didn't go home all n-night, and Miss Canning is worried. But she didn't r-report his absence, so I d-don't see how you c-come into the picture at all.'

'Because Detective Constable Worthington, who was on duty last night to report on Charlton's movements, was found dead this morning, not half a mile from the studio. And when we went there to look for Charlton the place was shut up, deserted. The corollary seems obvious – '

'Only to a b-bloody copper.'

It would have been hard to say at this stage which of them was the more furious. 'You must admit' – it was hard to tell whether Briggs was appealing to Sir Nicholas or to Vera, who was standing all this time close by her husband's side – 'Mr Maitland's attitude does nothing to dispel the impression I have of his part in the affair.'

'As I take it you have made these accusations entirely without grounds,' said Sir Nicholas at his silkiest, 'I think it would be – let us say – tactful to forget them for the moment. That is good advice, Chief Superintendent, whether you are in a condition to recognise it as such or not,' he added, and now there was no mistaking the steel behind the words. Briggs blinked once, but evidently decided he had gone far enough.

'At least, Sir Nicholas, you will agree that my request to see Miss Canning is a reasonable one.'

'So long as you do so in my presence.' He held up a hand as Briggs seemed about to expostulate. 'Miss Canning is a very young lady, and since she has taken refuge in my house I must hold myself in some degree responsible for her. Will you fetch Clare, Antony?'

No use arguing with Uncle Nick in this mood. Perhaps, in any event, he was in the right of it. Maitland had taken no more than two steps towards the door before he was halted by Briggs's voice . . . more pompous than ever, he thought unkindly.

'There can certainly be no objection to your presence, Sir Nicholas. I cannot help feeling that it will be more helpful than Mr Maitland's, for instance. But if Miss Canning, as I gathered from something that was said, is already in Mr Maitland's own quarters, I should prefer to see her there.'

Sir Nicholas glanced at his nephew. It would have been hard

to tell the direction of his thoughts. 'What have you to say to that, Antony?'

'You won't find Charlton there, if that's what you're thinking.' For the moment he was conscious only of weariness and of the pain in his shoulder. His uncle held his eyes for a second or two more, then he turned away and said brusquely:

'Very well then, I take it we have your permission,' and went to the door and held it open for the two detectives to precede him into the hall.

As soon as the door had closed behind them, Vera went across to the fireplace. 'Come and sit down,' she invited. Truth to tell, Antony had a pallor that alarmed her, but when he did not immediately reply she went on challengingly, 'Or are you too angry?'

He moved then, but only to stand with his left hand on the mantel, looking down at her where she had seated herself at the right of the hearth. 'As a matter of fact,' he said, and was surprised as he spoke that he was giving her so much honesty, 'I'm too scared to be angry any longer.'

'That man . . . Briggs . . . doesn't like you. Obvious enough.'

'It isn't that. But – didn't you see? – even Uncle Nick wondered for a moment – '

'Imagining things,' said Vera stoutly. Antony smiled at her absently, but went on as if she hadn't spoken.

'He'd believe me, I think, if I assured him when we were alone that I'd nothing to do with Charlton's disappearance.' He paused, and a rather startled look crept into his eyes. 'At least, I hope that's true. Heaven and earth, Vera, I'd have had more sense from Charlton's point of view, let alone my own. But I don't know that Uncle Nick trusts me not to lie to Briggs.'

This time Vera did not attempt to argue. 'Why does he dislike you so?' she asked.

'It's . . . I can't think of any better phrase than mutual antipathy, and that's trite enough,' said Antony in a dissatisfied tone. 'Uncle Nick would say it's my own fault, I lost my temper once too often in the early days of our acquaintance, and ever since . . . well, since our last dust up, five or six years ago, I thought he'd resigned himself to the fact of my honesty, but this is something new.'

'How d'you mean?'

'You know the charge against Harry Charlton, don't you? The original charge, before all this talk of murder.'

'Offence under the Official Secrets Act,' said Vera. '*Now* the implication seems to be that he's in the process of defecting.'

'Yes, and that spells treason in anybody's book, whatever the law calls it. I didn't think even Briggs would suspect me of having a hand in anything like that.'

'See what you mean. But I think, to do him justice, that the Chief Superintendent's main concern was the murder of this man, Worthington. He thought when you heard about that you'd be willing to tell him all you knew.'

'That's not much consolation.'

Vera gave him one of her searching looks. 'More than that, isn't there?'

'Uncle Nick – '

'Don't worry what Nicholas thinks. He knows well enough that you believe Harry Charlton is innocent.'

'Yes, but . . . he objects to the – the unfriendly attentions of the police almost as bitterly as Gibbs does; what's more, he says it's my own fault for having got off on the wrong foot with Briggs in the first place, and that's fair enough comment. But I told you that. What I'm driving at is that this time I've involved you too; if you'd seen his face when he came through that door and saw you here with us – '

'Did see it,' said Vera, and gave a sudden, unexpected bark of laughter. 'He knows by now I'm not a clinging vine,' she added, with one of her reversions to the phraseology of her girlhood, and got up purposefully. 'Get you a drink,' she said, and crossed the hearth to ring the bell at the other side of the fireplace, a thing none of the other members of the household had dared to do for years.

III

It was about twenty minutes later that they heard voices in the hall. 'Going to say goodbye to your friends?' asked Vera, and Antony, a little relaxed now, grimaced at her over the rim of his glass. He got to his feet as the sounds of departure faded, and was facing the door when Sir Nicholas came into the room.

'Are they gone?' he asked, unnecessarily.

'They are.' Sir Nicholas's tone was grim, but his attention was not yet upon his nephew. His eyes sought his wife's. 'I'm sorry you were subjected to that rather unedifying scene,' he said.

'Own fault,' said Vera tersely. 'Curious,' she added and saw, as she had hoped, a faint lightening of the severity of his expression.

'I hope Antony has made his apologies,' he said. Vera only smiled. Antony said, against his better judgment because he knew his uncle hated to be rushed:

'Clare – ?'

Sir Nicholas came over to his own chair, and seated himself in his leisurely way. 'I see you have been fortifying yourself against my coming,' he said.

'My idea,' said Vera, and 'Don't you think it was a good one?' said Maitland, almost in the same breath.

'In the circumstances, an excellent idea.' Sir Nicholas's voice had still that dangerous gentleness. 'You will perhaps explain to me why the disappearance of one of your clients should bring the police immediately to our doorstep.'

'Uncle Nick, I'm sorry.'

'Your state of mind does not interest me. I asked you a question.'

'I have no explanation. How can I explain to you what I don't understand myself?'

'You will perhaps remember that I warned you there might be trouble with Briggs.'

'Of course I remember! Look, you've got to tell me, sir, how is Clare?'

This time Sir Nicholas condescended to answer the question. 'Clare is a good girl, and is displaying considerably less emotion than I might have expected from your rather hysterical account of her condition.'

No use taking time to dispute the fairness of this. 'Briggs didn't upset her?'

'I hope I know by now how to protect a witness, Antony. Clare will do very well. Jenny, however – '

'Uncle Nick!'

'Nothing was said openly, of course, but I believe she realised the implications of the Chief Superintendent's visit as well as if they had been spelled out for her.'

'I'd better go.'

'Not until you have told me what you mean to do.'

'Follow the few leads I have. I've no hope they'll lead me to Harry Charlton, however . . . if he's alive.'

'You persist in this touching belief in his innocence?'

'Nothing that has happened has changed my mind about that.'

'Even the death of this unfortunate policeman.'

'Even that. If someone kidnapped him they'd have had to dispose of the policeman somehow.'

'It seems so much more likely, however – ' He looked across at Vera. 'Have you tried reasoning with him, my dear?'

'Not at all sure which way reason lies,' said Vera at her gruffest.

That momentarily silenced Sir Nicholas. Not without a certain reprehensible satisfaction, Maitland asked him, 'Did you satisfy yourself that Harry Charlton wasn't concealed anywhere about the premises?' and it must be admitted that he did not attempt to soften the inflection of sarcasm in his tone.

Sir Nicholas did not answer that immediately. He was eyeing his nephew rather as though he had never seen him before.

Then he said, still mildly, 'Your word has always been good enough for me, Antony.'

'I'm relieved to hear it, sir. Briggs, however – ' He broke off as a thought struck him and then went on, speaking more quickly than before. 'You said Jenny got the implications of his visit. You don't mean he searched the place?'

His uncle permitted himself a faint, austere smile. 'That I should not have countenanced,' he said. 'However, Jenny's manner, and Clare's too, would have convinced even a more sceptical man than Briggs.' He paused there, perhaps waiting for some comment, and then added in the gentle tone that Maitland disliked so much, 'Don't deceive yourself, Antony. We haven't succeeded in persuading him that you aren't somehow involved in Charlton's disappearance.'

'I suppose I should thank you for that "we",' said Antony bitterly. He gave that a moment or two to sink in. 'Have you anything else you want to say to me, Uncle Nick?'

If Sir Nicholas recognised the appeal in that he gave no sign of it. 'Would anything I can say convince you that you should keep out of the matter now?' he enquired. 'Confine yourself to representing Charlton, if he returns.'

'There's Clare to think of.'

'If Charlton is a double murderer, besides being guilty of some treasonable activities, you will do Clare no favour by restoring him to her.' He turned suddenly to Vera. 'You must agree with me in this at least.'

Vera shared one of her grim smiles between them. 'As the proposition is put . . . yes, of course I agree with you, Nicholas. But there's Antony's point too : if the man is innocent – '

'I'd put it stronger than that: because he's innocent,' said Maitland rashly. Sir Nicholas surveyed him with a cold eye.

'I shall say no more,' he announced. Antony looked at him a moment longer, not altogether trusting this statement, and then turned and went out without another word.

When his nephew had gone Sir Nicholas sat for a short time gazing after him, then he sighed and got up to attend to the fire. Vera was willing enough to let him take his time about speaking, but when he seated himself again rather heavily, as though he were feeling his years, she began to look anxious. But still she left it to her husband to break the silence, and when he said, 'I'm glad he had the grace to apologise to you, Vera,' she did not correct the assumption. Only when he added, with a gleam in his eye that might almost have been amusement, 'I don't know why I bother,' did she say, at her most elliptical:

'Can tell you that. Danger.'

'You're right, of course. And there's the further complication of Briggs's attitude. Which I don't understand,' he added thoughtfully.

'Told me they never got on.'

'That's true enough. All the same, there's Antony's war record . . . don't tell me Briggs isn't perfectly well aware of everything that's ever happened to him. And now to imply that he might be mixed up in something that smacks of espionage – '

'No implication about it,' Vera corrected him. 'Said it right out.'

'That doesn't make it any better,' said Sir Nicholas ruefully. 'But you will admit, my dear, it's a puzzle.'

'Told him myself once he'd get himself disbarred one of these days,' said Vera. To anybody else it might have seemed an odd sort of comfort, but it is a fact that her husband seemed cheered by this rather gloomy statement.

'If it hasn't happened so far,' he said quite hopefully, 'it probably never will.' And got up to serve them both from the tray that Gibbs had provided half an hour before.

IV

His talk with Sir Nicholas had filled Antony with foreboding, but Jenny displayed only her usual serenity when she heard the door and came into the hall to greet him. Secretly, she was shocked by his appearance, but she had arranged with

102

herself years ago never to refer by word or look to the fact that she could tell when his shoulder was more painful than usual; and now she supposed, a little sadly, that the same resolve might well cover his rather sick pallor and general air of bewilderment. 'I made Clare lie down,' she said. 'If you want anything from the bedroom I can get it for you. And I've got those addresses you wanted, so as soon as we've had lunch – '

He ignored the mention of food, unless the look of revulsion that crossed his face could be construed as a comment. 'Thank you, love,' he said. And then, more urgently, 'Did he upset her? Or you?' Jenny was in no danger of believing that the second query was really an afterthought.

'With Uncle Nick here? Of course not. But he was angry, Antony, wasn't he? I suppose that was with you.'

'Whether you mean Uncle Nick or Briggs, it was with me.' He put his left arm round her shoulder and steered her through the open door of the living-room. When he released her she went to her usual corner of the sofa and he thought, with a momentary pang, that it was the only thing that betrayed her tension . . . the prim way she seated herself, not looking relaxed at all. 'You do realise, Jenny – don't you? – I can't leave things as they are.'

'I know.' Without conscious thought she went to the heart of the query. 'Uncle Nick doesn't agree with you.'

'That's the least of my worries.'

'He'll get over it,' said Jenny, answering the spirit and not the letter of what was said.

'I'm not so sure, love. However – '

'There's something else, isn't there?' she asked when he did not seem inclined to finish the sentence. And he said to her simply, as he had said to Vera:

'I'm scared.' The sound of his own voice startled him. He could remember many occasions in the past when he had been afraid, but none on which he had been willing to admit the fact, even to Jenny. And now, twice within half an hour . . .

'Of Superintendent Briggs?' She sounded incredulous.

'Of the effect a scandal could have on all of us. But that isn't all, Jenny. I seem to be forgetting all my good resolutions about keeping you in the dark,' he added, and the bewilderment was in his voice now, as well as in his eyes.

'They aren't very good resolutions, Antony. I'd rather know.'

'I'm beginning to realise that.' (And you have the sort of courage I can only aspire to.) 'You see, love, it's . . . the other side.'

'You mean . . . "them"?' asked Jenny, perfectly seriously.

'If Charlton has been kidnapped . . . Clare can't hear us, can she?'

'She was nearly asleep when I left her. In any case, we'd have heard the bedroom door.'

'Good. Well, if *that* has happened, it's probably to clinch the idea of his guilt in the mind of the authorities, and to discourage me from persisting with my enquiries. Don't you think there'll be some reaction when they find I'm pressing on regardless?'

'It's obvious, of course.' She said that steadily, and took a moment to admire, almost cold-bloodedly, her own air of unconcern. But then she looked up and found, unexpectedly, that he was laughing at her, and joined in his laughter with a sense of release. 'And that's what's upsetting Uncle Nick, Antony. Not anything else.'

He was serious in an instant. 'I doubt that, love, but let's wait and see. I ought to be going.'

'And I can't leave Clare.' She didn't mention lunch again, having a pretty good idea what his reaction would be. 'Before you go, Antony . . . that other man.'

He frowned over that for an instant, but of course it should have been obvious. 'Wylie?' he said.

'Something like that. From the Special Branch anyway. He fell behind when they were leaving and said he'd like to talk to you again.'

'That was pretty good cheek.'

'He didn't sound unfriendly. And he asked if you'd be at home this evening.'

'I don't know where I'll be. I'll call you, Jenny, if I get delayed. And if Wylie wants to see me . . . well, they're calling the shots. I don't seem to have much choice.' He stretched out a hand to pull her to her feet. 'Don't worry about my activities this afternoon, love. And, console yourself, if we do get a reaction later on it will mean we're on the right track.'

Jenny went with him to the door and stood there a moment listening as his footsteps grew fainter on the stairs. She was wondering, a trifle forlornly, exactly what he meant by reaction, but after a moment she stiffened her shoulders, shut the door firmly, and went off to the kitchen to survey her ruined soufflé.

V

It wasn't until he got down into the hall that he stopped to check the list of addresses Jenny had given him. It wasn't an area that he was familiar with, but Basil had said he could take the Piccadilly line to South Ealing, and presumably from there a cab driver could put him straight. Always provided he had enough cash on him, but when he checked that seemed to be all right. He could hear the faint murmur of talk from the study, and resisted the impulse to interrupt it. There was nothing he could say or do at this point to make matters any better. Get on with the business at hand then. If only the whole thing didn't seem so hopeless, so much of an effort.

The day had started out warm and sunny. He hadn't noticed that it had clouded over and a brisk wind had sprung up. That might be all to the good, might serve to clear his head, but when he arrived at the Tube station he couldn't flatter himself that the walk had done him any good at all. And though he tried to concentrate on the problem of the coming interviews during the journey that followed, that wasn't very successful either. The aftermath of the scene with Briggs had left him feeling sick and shaken. If he had thought it possible that Harry Charlton was still alive he might have felt more sense of urgency. As it was . . .

And always there was the small, nagging thought that perhaps Briggs was right after all in his assessment of what had happened. Uncle Nick had agreed with him, hadn't he? And Uncle Nick was no fool. Perhaps he himself would have seen things differently if he hadn't wanted so desperately to help Clare.

He had expected difficulty, and perhaps some telephoning, before he got hold of a cab, but he was lucky in walking almost straight into one; and luckier still in the driver, who scanned his list of addresses knowledgeably. 'This chap's the nearest,' he said, pointing to Julian Shacklock's name. 'Take you there first, shall I?'

'And wait for me, if you don't mind.'

'Anything to oblige,' said the driver happily. His cheerfulness had the effect of making Antony delve into his wallet again. Perhaps he ought to have seen what cash Jenny had on her; but, no, all seemed to be well. Even if the journey was longer than he had anticipated . . .

Julian Shacklock's abode turned out to be one half of a red brick house of eccentric aspect. Antony, wondering for the first time whether he had come all this way for nothing, went up the short drive and pressed the bell.

No rather effete-sounding chimes here, a good healthy clatter. If that didn't get a response . . . but he needn't have worried. There was the briefest of pauses before the door was pulled open by a tall man, who appeared for a moment taken aback at finding a stranger on his doorstep.

'Mr Shacklock?'

'Yes.' Nothing in his tone but a sort of polite bewilderment.

Maitland introduced himself. 'I'm really here as a friend of Harry Charlton, rather than as his lawyer. You're aware, of course, of the position.'

'There was a short paragraph in my paper this morning.' Shacklock moved back and held the door wider. 'A dead man,

Harry's address was mentioned. Or was that just a coincidence?'

His mind was so full of more recent happenings that it took Antony a moment to remember Foster's murder, and to realise that the later murder and the disappearance of the suspect couldn't yet have appeared in the press. 'No coincidence,' he said, and stepped across the threshold into the hall. 'But as far as Charlton is concerned – '

'Yes, well, of course, you'd have to say that. I wonder if I'm wise to be talking to you.' He paused there, openly weighing up his visitor, and then shrugged and turned towards an open door on the right of the hall. 'You'd better come in.'

Once through the doorway into the room beyond it became obvious why he had chosen this rather old-fashioned maisonette rather than a modern luxury apartment. It was, quite simply, a handsome room, beautifully proportioned, and far larger than it had appeared from outside. As for the furnishings, Antony was only conscious that they complemented it perfectly, he couldn't afterwards have described them in any detail. But he took the chair that Shacklock indicated with a wave of his hand, and set himself conscientiously to study his host.

When he had stepped up into the hall their eyes had been level. Shacklock had auburn hair that a woman might have envied, worn fashionably long and slightly wavy. His features were regular, a good-looking chap, but not too handsome. He was dressed for comfort, a sweater over a sports shirt and slacks, but contrived at the same time to look almost excessively elegant. Antony, meeting his eyes, thought they were uncomfortably penetrating. No kind of a fool, but nobody working for Basil on that infernally complicated project . . .

'You're looking for an alternative to Harry Charlton's guilt,' said Shacklock, disconcerting him. 'I hope this visit doesn't mean I've been elected.'

No use to protest, he wouldn't be believed. 'I don't think Charlton has been guilty of anything worse than an indiscretion,' Maitland said deliberately. 'But I only want the truth.'

'How naïve of you.' Shacklock's amusement was perhaps a little more evident than was strictly polite. 'I mean, of course, to think that I should tell it you, if I were the source of the leak.' But he went on quickly, before Antony could speak, and now he seemed genuinely interested in getting an answer. 'You say the murder wasn't a coincidence. Doesn't even that shake your faith a little?'

'Not even that.' Not even the second murder and Charlton's disappearance, about which this man, if he were an innocent bystander, could know nothing yet. But even as he spoke he could hear his uncle's voice – 'This touching belief in his innocence' – and knew that any kind of confidence, let alone the kind of confidence he was protesting, was the last thing he could look for in this matter.

'Then what connected it with Harry? Besides the fact that the body was found in his garden?'

'Do you know any details of the case against him?'

'Not really.'

'The dead man was one of the prosecution witnesses. *The* prosecution witness, really.'

Shacklock gave a low whistle of surprise. 'I never put Harry down as a cautious man, but surely the most elementary instinct of self-preservation – ' He broke off there, though he didn't seem like a man who would normally be at a loss for words.

'You'd think so, wouldn't you?' Maitland's tone was carefully non-committal. And suddenly the other man laughed, though the cause of his amusement was not immediately apparent.

'This opens up a new train of thought,' he said. 'Perhaps after all – ' But again he did not finish his sentence. Instead he got up purposefully. 'Can I offer you a drink?'

A stiff brandy might settle the feeling of nausea once and for all, but it was more important to keep a clear head. And as Shacklock appeared to be alone here he didn't want to interrupt the proceedings by asking for tea. 'Ginger ale, if you have it,' said Maitland firmly.

'Anything you say.' The cupboard in the corner proved to house a well-fitted, well-stocked bar. Shacklock poured scotch for himself, scrabbled for a moment in the depths of the cupboard until he found a can of ginger ale, added ice and placed the glass at Antony's elbow. 'Not my idea of hospitality,' he said, grimacing.

'I had no lunch,' said Maitland apologetically. The last thing he wanted at the moment was to do anything to disturb the other man's sudden friendliness.

'All right then.' Shacklock sipped his scotch appreciatively, set down the glass, and eyed his companion in an enquiring way. 'For the purposes of this conversation we are postulating Harry's innocence, though I shouldn't like you to think me a credulous man.'

'Not so credulous as I am, for instance,' said Maitland, and smiled, almost for the first time since Clare's arrival that morning.

'That's what I meant,' Shacklock admitted. 'The next question is, as I see it, do you also absolve Jim Rickover from blame?'

'He was to blame, of course, for talking to Charlton at all.'

'I am probably even more aware of that than you are, having invested so many years of my life in the project. But that wasn't what I meant.'

'No. My own instinct, though – and I'd be the first to admit it isn't always reliable – is that there's somebody else. I mean, if Rickover were selling secrets to the enemy, the last thing he would have done was to talk to Charlton as well.'

'That's an uncomfortable thought. You will forgive me if I say I prefer the police theory, and find it more credible too.'

'You agreed,' Antony reminded him, 'to accept my hypothesis for the moment.'

'So I did. What are your questions then?'

'Tell me about the Mariners' Arms.'

'I don't . . . well, it's just a pub. Rather a good one, I like it.'

'A pub that you, and some of your colleagues, frequent.'

'Yes, I suppose you would be interested in that.' But he

took a moment to think out the connection. Maitland made no attempt to enlighten him as to his own thoughts on the subject. He had a feeling that Shacklock was quite capable of working that out for himself. 'It isn't the only pub within strolling distance of the lab,' Shacklock went on. 'There's a more modern, road-house type of place that some of the chaps prefer, but a few of us like a more old-fashioned atmosphere, so naturally we come across each other there quite often.'

'By arrangement?'

'Accidentally, mostly. Of course, occasionally Vince and I – that's Vincent Brewer, the Chief of Guidance Systems – would be in the middle of an argument and go there to finish it. He's by way of being a friend of mine. A complete Philistine, of course, but still – '

'An argument about your work?' asked Maitland, intent now upon his witness.

Shacklock gave him a rather odd look, one at any rate that he couldn't interpret, and said with a touch of impatience, 'Of course not. To talk about our problems in public would in itself have been an infringement of security.'

'I see. Assuming Charlton's innocence for the moment, I'm most concerned with the people who had an overall knowledge of the project he was interested in.'

'Of whom I am one.'

'That, after all, is why I am here.'

'Well, you may have a point. Not about me, I'm afraid, but it's a fact that Harry couldn't have got much useful information from Jim. That might be a point you could make in court: if he were being paid by the Russians they'd expect something for their money.'

'I'll remember that,' said Maitland gravely.

Shacklock gave him a quick smile. 'I know, teaching my grandmother,' he said, but he was still intent on his argument. 'I can see why you're concentrating on those of us who knew the complete details of the project, but what has the Mariners' Arms got to do with it?'

'Because I think Harry Charlton has been deliberately

framed . . . it's the only thing that squares with his innocence.'

'If you realise that – ' Shacklock began, but Maitland was following his own train of thought and ignored the interruption.

'If that is so,' he said, and smiled himself fleetingly, thinking of Jenny and her unexpected incursion into his talk with Basil, 'if that is so it's most likely to have been done by someone who knew something of him personally.'

'I can't say I like the way the situation seems to be developing,' said Shacklock thoughtfully. 'You seem to be pretty well informed about all of us. Who was your informant?'

'Basil Vlasov, who is an old friend of mine.'

'Is he though? And what did he say when he saw the way your ideas were tending?'

'It was quite obvious that he feels all of you are above suspicion.'

'I'm glad to hear it. Let's see then, people who knew all the details of the project and were also in the habit of spending some time in the pub Harry chose for his investigations. Myself, of course, as you pointed out, not at all tactfully really; Basil; Vincent Brewer; and the redoubtable Mrs Edwards.'

'Basil?' said Antony, startled for a moment out of his cautious approach.

'Basil certainly. The whole thing's his brainchild, of course he knows all about it.'

'I hadn't realised he ever formed part of the group at the Mariners' Arms.'

'He goes there occasionally.' Shacklock had a sardonic look for his visitor's obvious surprise. 'I thought perhaps that was the object of the exercise, that you were checking up on him.'

Another comment that was best ignored. 'He tells me it was Mr Brewer who first pointed out to him what Harry Charlton was up to.'

'That's right, but I was there at the time. He didn't seem to have had any idea . . . well, that was fair enough, he didn't meet Harry as often as the rest of us.'

'But Mr Brewer and Mrs Edwards would have known?'

'Certainly. We were all rather amused by it really . . . no, I should exclude Vince from that, he had a more – I suppose in view of what's happened I should say a more responsible attitude than the rest of us.' He paused, and when he went on sounded for the first time completely serious. 'You know, we've all worked so hard and so long on this idea of Basil's that I don't think it occurred to any of us that someone might talk out of turn.'

'If I'm right, it occurred to somebody,' said Maitland sombrely. 'Tell me about Charlton, and his relationship with each of the people we've mentioned.'

'That's getting close to home again,' Shacklock complained, but the light tone was back. 'Apart from Jim Rickover – but we're absolving Jim, aren't we? – I was certainly the person on the most friendly terms with him.'

'How was that?'

'Interests in common. Harry is surprisingly knowledgeable about music, for one thing, opera in particular. And he manages to keep up with all the latest books and plays.'

'Those things don't appeal to the others?'

'I think Basil has a love of the ballet, but latterly he's been too preoccupied to spend much time in idle chatter. Vince has very little conversation that isn't technical.'

'You said – '

'Not our own stuff, we reserve that for the lab. Other people's projects, the little you read about them in the papers. As for Sheila, she's the open-air type. I don't think she had much time for Harry at all.'

'I understood Mr Brewer has some interest in politics.'

'Nothing that would endear him to Harry. Or *vice versa*. He's a bit right-wing for most of our tastes, as a matter of fact, but that's probably reaction from a . . . from his marriage.'

'You were going to qualify that in some way.'

'All right, as I seem to be being frank with you. I was going to say, from a disastrous marriage. I only meant that he

112

married a brilliant woman, and for all her good looks I find her a dead bore.'

'Does Mr Brewer also regard his marriage as disastrous?'

'Heavens, no. Just the opposite. Uxorious,' said Shacklock. And what was that but the bachelor's description of a happily married man? 'Looking back on it in the light of our premise, does it strike you that any of your colleagues took a more than ordinary interest in Harry Charlton?'

Shacklock obligingly gave that the benefit of a moment's thought. 'I can't say it does,' he said at last. 'It seemed like a good joke, and we weren't above playing up to him . . . all of us except Vince.'

'I see.' He realised that he was clutching his glass of ginger ale like a talisman, and drained it quickly. 'Do you know anything about a restaurant called Jenners'?' he asked, replacing the glass carefully on its coaster.

'Isn't that where Harry took Jim to pump him? That's all I know about it, I'm afraid.' He had an enquiring look, but even if he had been able to do so, Maitland didn't feel like trying to satisfy his curiosity.

'You've been uncommonly patient with me,' he said, coming to his feet.

Shacklock got up too. If he was eager to see the back of his visitor there was nothing in his manner to show it. 'I don't know whether I should wish you good luck,' he said. 'As I told you, I find your theories extremely uncomfortable.'

'Basil didn't like them either. Do you think I shall find your friends the Brewers at home?'

'Vince and Susan? I really haven't the faintest idea.'

'And Mrs Edwards?'

'On a fine Sunday? *She* won't be at home.'

'I can but try. I had meant to come to the laboratory tomorrow and see all of you there, but then something came up.' He did not attempt to elaborate on that.

'From what you tell me I take it,' said Shacklock, following him towards the door, 'that I had the doubtful distinction of being the first on your list.'

Maitland turned and smiled at him. He still wasn't feeling much like smiling, but the need to concentrate had steadied him, and he had himself pretty well under control again. 'The cab driver selected your address,' he said, 'as being the most convenient first port of call. Nothing more sinister than that.'

'I'm relieved to hear it.' Was that said sardonically, or was there a hint of genuine feeling there?

'Goodbye, Mr Shacklock, and thank you again,' said Antony, and pulled open the door and went out to his patient taxi.

VI

The next address the driver chose was that of Sheila Edwards, which proved to be a fairly modern, semi-detached house not far from Shacklock's place, and of a quite frightening mediocrity. But here his luck ran out, there was no one at home. For some reason this seemed an almost insurmountable setback, though it was only what he ought to have expected after all. He returned to his cab discomfited, the driver's cheerfulness was beginning to wear him down, but he hadn't much time to dwell on the reverse, the block of flats which apparently housed the Brewers was only a few minutes' drive away.

And here was the modern version of luxury that Shacklock had eschewed. There was a doorman, who insisted on announcing him, which gave him a moment's worry because he couldn't see himself making his explanations over the house phone, and through a third party at that. But all was well, Mr Brewer was in and would see him. He was given the flat number, on the eleventh floor, and made free of the lift.

Brewer was waiting for him when the gates opened. A man nearly as tall as Shacklock, but much more conventionally attired, with dark hair that was receding at the temples, a pleasantly craggy face, and brown eyes that for some reason seemed to be regarding him with sympathy. 'Mr Maitland?' he said.

'Yes. I'm sorry to disturb you on a Sunday.'

'That doesn't matter.' He was leading the way down the long, thickly carpeted corridor now. 'If I sounded surprised it's because Basil told me you'd be coming to the lab tomorrow.'

'Suddenly it didn't seem a very good idea to wait. But I shall have to come there anyway; Mrs Edwards was out when I called on her just now.'

'Well, yes, she would be. Here we are.' The open door led straight into an expensively furnished living-room. Maitland was more alert now, and would have been glad enough to compare it mentally with Julian Shacklock's own particular brand of luxury if only he had been in a fit state at the time of that visit to take in his surroundings. Still, he had the impression that here more money had been expended with less taste, but then he heard Brewer saying, 'Mr Maitland, Susan, Harry Charlton's lawyer. I told you Basil mentioned him when he phoned this morning.'

Rather to his embarrassment she rose to greet him, and offered him her hand. As he took it he was aware of surprise. Basil had mentioned charm, and Shacklock had said, 'for all her good looks', but there was that rarity, a woman of really classical beauty. Perhaps this fact was all the more startling because she seemed so unconscious of it. Her hair – nearly as fair as Clare's – was long and twisted up into a knot in a way no hairdresser would have countenanced, and the rather severely-cut suit she wore, while no doubt an excellent choice for the office, was completely unsuitable for a quiet Sunday afternoon at home.

'Rather a thankless task, Mr Maitland,' she said, and he could have sworn that she too had some sympathy for him. Brewer was regarding her in an infatuated way for which even Shacklock's remarks hadn't prepared him. 'Would you like me to leave you and Vincent alone?'

'No . . . please. I don't want to disturb you in any way. And this is quite informal. I expect,' he added hopefully, 'Basil explained that too.'

'I think I assumed it,' said Brewer easily. 'Sit down, Mr

Maitland.' His wife went back to her chair as he spoke. 'Can I get you a drink? Or would you like some tea, perhaps?'

Presumably, if he said Yes to that last offer, which he would dearly have liked to have done, Susan Brewer would leave them while she prepared it. And he had the feeling, strangely after so short a time together, that these two should be considered as one person, that if the wife left the room the husband would be so much less himself. 'Nothing for me, thank you,' he said. And then, softening the refusal, 'I've already spent some time this afternoon with Mr Shacklock.'

'Oh, Julian.' Antony thought she was trying for an indulgent tone, but it didn't quite come off. 'Then I can imagine you are in no further need of alcoholic refreshment.'

'Come now, Susan, you'll be persuading our friend that poor Julian is an alcoholic,' said Brewer in a rallying tone. 'Which is very far from being the case,' he added, seating himself in a chair from which he could keep both of his companions easily in view. Antony had the thought that this was a man never quite happy when his wife was out of his sight. 'A brilliant man,' Brewer went on, afraid that he would miss the point. 'But perhaps you could see that for yourself.'

'I take it you mean technically. I'm in no position to judge anybody on that score. But he used the word brilliant himself. Of you, Mrs Brewer.'

She took the compliment gracefully, but still there was the thread of malice in her reply. 'I don't imagine he meant that altogether kindly, Mr Maitland. Julian doesn't approve of women who step outside their traditional role.'

'I was interested in what Basil had to tell me about the very fine job you have made of *The Weekend Review*.' That was shameless flattery, but the point about his interest was true enough.

'Do you know it?' Luckily for him she didn't give him time to answer that. 'It's an important job, you know, though Vincent doesn't altogether approve.' Brewer looked deprecating.

'I'm sure it is.' Maitland had assumed an air of earnest

enquiry. 'What interests you most, Mrs Brewer? The literary side, or the political.'

'They both have their value. But it is the political angle that gives the *Review* its unique quality, Mr Maitland. That's the whole point of what we're trying to do . . . to enlighten the masses.'

For a so-called clever woman, he thought, that was a singularly trite remark; he also doubted whether the magazine had a wide enough distribution for it to be true. But before he could formulate another question Brewer laughed in a rather half-hearted way and said uneasily, 'Yes, well, that is a point on which we must agree to differ,' and suddenly she was laughing with him.

'You're quite right, of course, Mr Maitland hasn't come here to hear us argue.' But she cast a distinctly complacent look round the room as she spoke, so that Antony thought there were probably material compensations for her husband in a line of work of which he disapproved.

'I'm interested, you see,' he said, abandoning the topic, and speaking in the diffident tone that could be so misleading, 'in getting an insight into Charlton's relationship with your colleagues. From your side of the fence, I mean, because of course I've heard his side of it already.'

Vincent Brewer took his time to think that over, and after a moment Susan said into the silence, impatiently, 'There wasn't a relationship at all really, except with that dreary young man, Rickover.' Antony turned an enquiring eye on her and she added, less brusquely, 'Well, I only know what Vincent has told me really. Though I did meet Harry Charlton once.'

'What did you make of him?'

'Tiresomely full of himself.'

If there was one thing that Charlton wasn't, in Antony's view, it was that. He smiled at Mrs Brewer and asked lightly, 'Didn't he ask you any questions?'

She had a wry look for that, perhaps she had a sense of humour after all. 'Dozens of them. By the time we'd been together half an hour he must have known as much about running a magazine as I do myself.'

'No personal questions?'

'They'd have come next, I expect, but Vincent took me away.'

'That meeting was at the Mariners' Arms?'

'Yes. I went there for a drink with Vincent before we went on to a meeting.'

Maitland would have liked to ask her, 'What sort of a meeting?' but there was a limit, he felt, beyond which it would not be wise to push her. Not a political meeting, presumably, since their views on that subject differed so greatly. Instead he turned to her husband. 'Is your opinion of Harry Charlton equally unfavourable?'

Brewer was apologetic. 'I think Basil said you were a friend of Charlton's.' Something in his distress reminded Maitland that both Vlasov and Shacklock had expressed a liking for this man, which now he felt he could understand very well.

'All the same,' he said, 'I should like to know what you thought of him.'

'He didn't worry me much. As Susan says, he had most to do with Jim Rickover, perhaps because they were much of an age. And I dare say he didn't realise there were limits to Jim's knowledge of the project. Otherwise, I'd say he talked mainly to Julian, books and plays. Frivolous stuff,' said Brewer, suddenly as much in earnest as his wife had been when she talked of her job. 'Give me a book with some meat in it, or play with a message.'

At this point Antony would very much have liked to go over and examine the bookshelves, but that too, in his estimation, went beyond the bounds of what was possible. 'Apart from these casual conversations, did any of your colleagues seem to take a particular interest in Charlton?'

'There was a good deal of talk about him in his absence. Most of them seemed to think it a good joke that he should be trying to pump us about a Top Secret project.'

'His intentions were common knowledge, then?'

'I can't say he was really subtle about it.'

'But *you* didn't think that was cause for amusement?'

'It was a serious business.'

'Basil tells me it was you who first put him wise to what was going on.'

'I felt he should know. Julian was there, and he made light of the matter. He is a friend of ours, but there are times – and that was one of them – when I lose all patience with him.' (Two such very different people, that wasn't really surprising.)

'How did Basil take the news?'

'Less seriously than I had hoped.'

'That was probably due to Julian's presence,' Susan Brewer put in. 'It would have been better to choose a time when you were alone with Basil.'

'I see that now.'

'But there was nothing – was there? – that Basil could have done about the situation. Short of putting the Mariners' Arms out of bounds to his staff, which I should think was hardly practicable.'

'He could have warned Jim of the dangers of that association.'

Maitland frowned over that. 'Are you telling me you foresaw what happened?'

'I think now I should have done,' said Brewer heavily.

Before Antony could reply to that, Susan said quickly, 'You can't blame yourself, Vincent, you couldn't have known.' Her husband turned and smiled at her.

'*You* may not blame me, but that doesn't mean I don't have some qualms about what happened,' he said. 'I saw more of Charlton than Basil did, and as the senior member of the group – '

'That's nonsense, and you know it. You couldn't have known,' said Susan again, stubbornly.

'It has been pointed out to me – you mentioned it yourself just now,' said Maitland, 'that Jim Rickover wasn't the best source of information that Charlton could have found.'

'His knowledge of the project was limited, but – as I think

I also pointed out to you – Charlton was probably not aware of that.'

'If he was gathering information to pass on to an enemy agent, he would have made it his business to be aware of it.'

That brought a moment of complete silence. Both Vincent and Susan Brewer seemed to be considering the implications of that, and not liking them, perhaps, any more than Julian Shacklock had done. 'There is just one more question,' Antony said, 'and it's not a very important one.' He thought afterwards he shouldn't have said that . . . like starting a sentence, 'To tell the truth' when you have no intention of doing so. His companions were looking expectant. 'What do you know about a restaurant called Jenners'?' he asked.

That came as an anticlimax, he could see that, and wondered what subtlety they had been anticipating. 'Nothing at all, except that it's where Harry Charlton used to meet his contact,' Brewer told him, and almost before he had finished his wife was on her feet, saying briskly:

'I'm going to make some tea now. You'll stay, won't you, Mr Maitland?'

'That's kind of you. If it's no trouble.'

The tea when it came was very good. Darjeeling, he thought. The conversation ranged while they drank it, but he did not attempt to bring it back to Harry Charlton again; and on the whole when he left it was with the feeling that it had been a wasted half-hour.

VII

Back at home, as he might have expected, he found Vera and Sir Nicholas taking tea with Jenny. That was another of the traditions, tea on Sundays when Uncle Nick was at home, but Antony realised when he went into the upstairs hall and heard their voices that on this occasion he had been anticipating a break with the past. The bedroom door was closed, and he wondered whether Clare was still sleeping, but when, after a

120

moment's hesitation, he pushed open the door to the living-room she was sitting with the rest of them, beside Jenny on the sofa.

Taking in the scene it was hard to believe that earlier in the day so much emotion had been generated. Sir Nicholas in his usual chair, as relaxed as ever he had seen him; Vera, sitting opposite him, looking exactly like herself, solid and depend-able; Clare, very still and quiet, but perfectly composed . . . but was it not rather her earlier agitation that had been out of character; and Jenny, still sitting primly (Uncle Nick would know what that meant well enough) with her teacup balanced precariously on the arm of the sofa.

It was Jenny who heard him come in and turned her head to smile at him. 'I'll make you some more tea,' she offered.

'Don't bother, love, I've had some.' He glanced from Vera to his uncle, said in a tone that was carefully unemotional, 'I'm sorry I couldn't get here before,' and then turned to Clare. 'How are you feeling now?'

'Better. I'm sorry I was so – so stupid,' she told him. And then, eagerly, 'Jenny told me you were seeing some of the people at the Fenton Laboratory who might really have done what Harry is accused of doing.'

Sir Nicholas, who had greeted his nephew's apology with a slight inclination of the head, stirred to life at that. 'If you gathered so much from Jenny's discourse, I must say I envy you your perspicacity,' he said. Clare, who was used to his ways and to being treated as one of the family, seemed rather cheered than otherwise by this speech; it was only Antony, with his unprecedented sensitivity to his uncle's moods, who wondered what lay behind it.

'All the same,' he said, 'it's near enough the truth.'

'Thing is,' Vera put in, 'did you have any luck?'

'Not so as you'd notice it.' He found Sir Nicholas's eyes fixed on him, and added uneasily, 'There were three people I wanted to see, and only two of them were at home.' There was a pause, while each of his audience considered that in his or her own way, so that after waiting in vain for some reaction

121

to his remark he grinned, though rather half-heartedly, and went on, 'I expect Jenny explained that to you too.'

'I did,' said Jenny, not at all resenting the implied slur on her powers of exposition. 'I told them all about your talk with Basil last night and what you deduced from it.'

'If I remember rightly, love, it was you who did the deducing.' He caught his uncle's eye again and added deliberately, 'Do you by any chance want to hear an account of two very inconclusive interviews?'

Sir Nicholas merely inclined his head once more. Vera said candidly, 'Why we waited for you,' so that Antony grinned again, with something like genuine amusement this time, and moved from his place on the hearthrug.

'Let's clear all this away, Jenny,' he said, piling cups and plates together in a determined way. 'Then we can all have a drink while I tell you. But you won't find it a particularly enthralling story, Uncle Nick. I only wish it were.'

VIII

It wasn't until after Vera and Sir Nicholas had gone that Jenny told him, 'That Inspector Wylie phoned, luckily before they got here. He said he'd come round about seven, and take a chance at finding you in.'

'It must be nearly that now.' Antony glanced at his watch, but it only confirmed his forebodings. 'Can we have dinner as soon as he's gone, love? I'm famished.'

'Of course, I – ' But before she could finish they were interrupted by the sound of the house phone. Jenny went to answer it, and when she came back announced simply, 'He's here.'

'I can't think,' said Antony, a little fretfully, 'why Gibbs has suddenly taken to using that instrument after all these years.'

'Vera's influence, I expect.' Jenny knew perfectly well that the subject wasn't one in which her husband had the slightest

122

interest at the moment. 'Come along, Clare,' she added. 'You can help me in the kitchen.' Clare got up obediently and followed her; Antony was pretty sure she was upset by the inconclusive nature of his recital, but there was nothing he could do about that. He went to open the hall door.

'I can't think what you want to see me for again,' he said disagreeably as Wylie came into sight round the bend in the stairs.

The Special Branch man made no immediate reply to that. He reached the landing, gave Maitland a rather intent look, and followed him into the living-room, still without speaking. 'Perhaps you weren't convinced this morning that Harry Charlton isn't here,' said Antony abruptly.

Wylie had a smile for that. It changed his appearance a good deal for the better. 'A quiet talk,' he said, going to Sir Nicholas's chair and seating himself uninvited.

'Wasn't enough said this morning?'

'I thought if we could be alone together something useful might emerge. If you will forgive me for saying so, Mr Maitland, you seem to have the knack of making yourself unpopular with the police.'

Antony came across to the hearth and leaned one shoulder against the mantel. The casual pose wasn't very convincing. 'Even Conway wouldn't have made the accusations that Briggs made this morning,' he said, speaking his thought without his usual caution. Rather to his discomfort, Wylie took up the subject as if he had been waiting for an opportunity to do so.

'You're thinking that the fact that Harry Charlton is a traitor should protect you from any suspicion of being involved with him.'

'Harry Charlton hasn't been convicted,' said Antony flatly.

'And is probably beyond our jurisdiction by now. But that wasn't the point I wanted to make, Mr Maitland. With your record – '

'Let's leave my record out of this, shall we?'

'I happen to have heard this and that about you,' said Wylie, impervious to the appeal. 'But things have changed

123

since you were in my line of business. *Then* the Russians were our allies.'

That brought Maitland upright in a flash. 'Now you're beginning to interest me,' he said. And added, when the other man made no immediate attempt to answer him, 'You can't leave it there, you know.'

'It seems to me I've said enough. Are you telling me you don't understand me?'

'You're implying – '

'Not I, Mr Maitland. I'm telling you what's being said, that's all.'

'And what is being said?' He was speaking quietly, in as gentle a tone as ever his uncle used when he was annoyed, but Wylie thought that for the first time he could understand what he knew of his companion's background. Maitland looked dangerous, far more dangerous than when he had lost his temper with the Chief Superintendent earlier in the day.

'That Communism and Fascism are at opposite ends of the spectrum.' Wylie, very much at his ease, spread his hands as though disclaiming responsibility for what he was saying.

'I . . . see.' Maitland was still speaking with that dangerous calmness, but his voice shook a little as he went on. 'Is that what you c-came here to t-tell me, Inspector Wylie? Or did you hope I'd be shocked into s-some sort of an admission?'

'I felt you ought to be aware – '

'R-rubbish.' He gave a short bark of laughter, completely unamused. 'I'm not simple enough to think you a simple man, Inspector. You have some devious reason of your own.'

'I hoped – I'll admit that if you like – that the knowledge might induce a certain candour in you.' Wylie's air of sincerity was blatantly overdone. Antony laughed again and flung himself down in the chair opposite his visitor.

'But what can you conceivably have to ask me that hasn't been asked already?' he enquired.

'You have some relationship with Charlton beyond the ordinary one of lawyer and client.'

124

'I thought Briggs had explained that,' said Maitland in a hard tone.

'Not altogether to my satisfaction.' Wylie, who hadn't impressed Antony as a cautious man, seemed now to be picking his words.

'You are too kind.' That was said sardonically, and to his surprise Wylie seemed distressed by it.

'I'm trying to be honest with you,' he said in a hurt tone.

'You can't blame me for doubting that, can you now?' But suddenly he relented. 'There's no great secret about it, anyway. The connection between Charlton and myself, such as it is, is based on my long-standing affection for Miss Canning.'

'You say, "such as it is," but you're putting yourself out on his behalf, aren't you, beyond what is customary?'

'Now, what do you know about that, Inspector?'

'Frankly, not so much as I should like. But I do know you entertained Mr Basil Vlasov at dinner last night.'

'Now, look here – '

'Before you get angry again, Mr Maitland, perhaps you'll let me explain. I wanted to get in touch with Mr Vlasov myself, and his housekeeper told me where he was.'

'Oh. Oh, I see.'

'And that's really why I'm here, Mr Maitland.' Wylie was oozing sincerity again, and the repeated use of his name was beginning to get on Antony's nerves. 'I've heard it said that you're discerning where people are concerned. What did you make of your visitor?'

Antony got up. Surely here, in his own room, he had a right to prowl if he wanted to, and if his movements disturbed the man from the Special Branch (who had managed without any apparent effort to disconcert him) so much the better. He went across to the window, paused there for a moment, and then came back and stood looking down at his companion. 'If you're really serious about that question it can only mean you're not altogether satisfied in your own mind about Charlton's guilt. Unless . . . I hadn't thought of that . . . unless you're checking up on my contacts. Which is it?'

'Take your pick, Mr Maitland.' Wylie sounded blandly self-satisfied. 'And when you've decided, I hope you'll answer my question.'

'Give me one good reason why I should.'

'To persuade me, perhaps, that we're on the same side of the fence.'

That sent Antony back to the window again. 'I've known Basil for years,' he said, speaking without turning his head from an apparent contemplation of the square below. 'More accurately, I knew him very well indeed for a short time about fourteen years ago, and then lost touch with him.' He swung round then, coming back to the hearth again and his unwelcome guest. 'If you want to know my opinion, he's utterly reliable.'

'People change in fourteen years.' (But haven't I been thinking just that, ever since my talk with Julian Shacklock this afternoon? If I'd been bright enough I might have inferred from what Basil said that he'd known Charlton, but the fact is, I didn't. I said last night, 'You're not a political animal,' but that's something that could have changed too; only in that case . . .)

'I believe you're being misled by his name, Inspector, though as you probably very well know his family have been here for ever,' said Antony, letting a certain amount of contempt creep into his voice. 'I should have thought, with your experience, you'd know better than that.'

Wylie did not attempt to answer this rather weak attempt at a counter-attack. 'What did you want of him?' he asked.

'To renew our acquaintance.'

'At this particular time?'

'I'd only just learned he was in London.' But seeing Wylie's sceptical look he went on, without more than a moment's pause, 'If you must have it, I wanted him to tell me the names of those of his associates who were better placed than Jim Rickover to give information to the enemy.'

'And you really think that one of them can lead you to Harry Charlton?'

Maitland gave him a rueful smile. 'I know it isn't likely,' he admitted. 'But it's the only line I've got. Unless you can suggest a better one,' he added hopefully.

'I think you're wasting your time,' said Wylie bluntly. 'It's all too clear, I can't understand why you can't see that.'

'Yes, let's talk about the case against Harry Charlton for a moment.' Antony sounded enthusiastic suddenly, and the other man gave him a suspicious look. 'You'd say it was a strong case, wouldn't you? The original charge, I mean, that he passed over some information to that friend of his, Vladimir Solovki.'

'I don't see your point, Mr Maitland. Of course it was a strong case.'

'Then why didn't you oppose bail? Tell me that, Inspector?'

'There's no reason, you know, why I should tell you anything at all.' If anything, Wylie seemed amused by this rather peremptory demand.

'Then *I'll* tell you. You thought he might have other associates, of whom you knew nothing, you were as conscious as I am that Rickover wasn't the best source of information. And you thought Charlton might lead you to somebody more important if he were at liberty.'

Briggs or Conway would certainly have said at this stage something like, 'I'm not here to play guessing games.' Wylie merely shook his head, in a thoughtful rather than a negative way, and said slowly, 'I should be interested to know where that conclusion leads you, Mr Maitland.' But his eyes were alert; to Antony he looked more like a fox terrier than ever.

'Don't tell me you're not there before me. You had him followed . . . it would be your people at that stage, not the C.I.D. So the question is, Inspector, where the hell was your man the night of Foster's murder?'

Wylie seemed to have tired for the moment of equivocating. 'I was wondering that myself when we first met at the studio,' he admitted. 'Of course, later on it became obvious, and taken in conjunction with what happened last night you might say a pattern began to emerge.'

'I might, if I had the faintest idea what you're talking about.'

'The man who was following Harry Charlton last night when he decided to disappear was found dead today.'

'So Briggs said.' But as the implications of what had been said sank in he added sharply, 'Don't tell me your chap is dead too!'

'Fortunately not. Only suffering from the effects of a blow on the head that caused temporary amnesia. That's why we weren't advised what had happened, he couldn't remember who he was or what he'd been doing when he woke up in hospital.'

'You said "temporary amnesia",' said Antony, pouncing on the point that interested him. 'What did he say later, when his memory returned to him?'

'Charlton left the studio at twenty-seven minutes past eight, with Meredith following, of course, and if he was going to the Dove and Pelican, as he says, he was going by a circuitous route. There weren't many people about, Meredith had to keep well back, then suddenly he went round a corner expecting to see Charlton ahead of him, but there was no one there. He went forward more quickly, heard a movement behind him, and then there was the blow.'

'Where was he found?'

'He'd been dragged into Landers Mews. That must be where Charlton had concealed himself.'

Antony felt a sudden stab of excitement, unwarrantable perhaps, but for the first time, if only momentarily, he felt the faint stirring of hope. 'When?' he asked sharply.

'Just before midnight. It isn't a residential mews, Mr Maitland, it isn't really surprising – '

'Isn't it? I can't agree with you there, Inspector. Who found him?'

'A man called Richardson, going to garage his car.'

'I don't suppose his is the only car kept there.'

'There are six garages.'

'And has any enquiry been made of the other tenants,

128

whether they were in or out between eight-thirty and midnight?'

There was no trace of amusement about Wylie now. 'Why should any such enquiry have been made?' he demanded.

Maitland made a wide, dissatisfied gesture. 'Because it's all too damned convenient,' he said.

'I don't understand you. Charlton knew he was being followed – '

'I don't think the fact had ever occurred to him, but leave that aside for the moment. When he was actually making his getaway – this is your theory, not mine – I suppose it wouldn't have mattered leaving the odd dead body strewn about the place; but on Friday night, when he was going straight home again – '

'After killing Foster.'

'That's just the point, don't you think? The discovery of your man, injured, would have been an additional strike against him. It would have been so easy . . . if you know you're being followed, it isn't too difficult to shake a tail.'

'You're trying to tell me that somebody else – '

'I'm going further than that. I'll acquit the C.I.D. man, because he's dead, but I think the other had, at the least, guilty knowledge of what was to be done that night.'

Wylie got slowly to his feet. He looked a little like a man who has been winded by an unexpected blow. 'I think you haven't seriously considered the implications of what you're saying, Mr Maitland.'

'I can't prove anything, of course.' Antony's airy tone made that sound like the most unimportant of details. 'But can you tell me I haven't made you think you'd like to look a little further into the events of Friday night?'

'Meredith had certainly been hit over the head.'

'A sensible precaution,' said Maitland approvingly. 'But I don't suppose anybody thought to ask the doctor at what time he received the blow, probably he wouldn't have been able to tell anyway. Any more than you thought to question the tenants of the mews garages.'

E

'There was absolutely no need for any such enquiries to be made. And I don't agree with you now,' he added more strongly. 'This is the purest fantasy.'

'Think about it,' Antony advised. 'And meanwhile, tell me, was Meredith one of the men who searched the studio?'

'Why yes, he was.'

'And found the incriminating documents? And perhaps at the same time noted where Charlton kept his neckties? If you find he was on duty when Charlton and Miss Canning went out to lunch on Friday – which they tell me is the only time the tie could have been taken – wouldn't even that shake your confidence in him, Inspector?'

But Wylie had recovered his equanimity. 'An argument based on quicksand,' he said scornfully. But even as Antony admired the unlikely phrase he was wondering whether his companion was quite as confident as he was trying to sound.

'And if I should want to see your Mr Meredith?' he asked.

'There can be no need of that either, unless Charlton is charged with the murder of William Foster.'

'In that case he would be a witness for the prosecution, and I should be prohibited from interviewing him. But meanwhile, with Harry Charlton missing – '

Again Wylie did not allow him to finish. 'Considering all things, I admire your gall,' he said, and laughed surprisingly. 'But it might be instructive at that.'

'That,' said Antony, watching his face, 'is the object of the exercise.'

'I was looking at it from my own point of view, not yours. If you don't mind my sitting in on the interview – ?'

Now what was the man up to? The last thing he had expected had been any sort of agreement with what, from where Wylie was sitting, must seem a pretty outrageous request. Not without some further argument. 'That would suit me very well, Inspector,' he said, concealing well enough a certain nervousness.

'Amusing, as well as instructive,' said Wylie, and to Mait-

130

land's relief began to move towards the door. 'I'll phone you tomorrow, shall I, when I see what can be arranged?'

'I'll be out in the morning, but I hope to be home for lunch.'

Antony went downstairs, to see the visitor safely off the premises, and heard again, as he closed the front door and went back across the hall, the sound of voices from the study in companionable conversation. He ought to tell Uncle Nick what Wylie had had to say to him, but perhaps that would be only to disturb again the uneasy balance of their relationship. His excitement of a few minutes before had left him now. He was tired, and his shoulder was playing up, and Jenny would be waiting for him. But as he began to climb the stairs he was guiltily conscious of the fact that if there was one thing more than another that his uncle disliked it was being kept in the dark.

IX

After his earlier abstinence he had a good dinner, and felt guilty all over again because Clare did very little but push her food round her plate. After the meal was over they sat in silence with their coffee for a while, until about nine o'clock when Clare got up resolutely and said, 'I think, if you don't mind, I'll go to bed.' She glanced at Antony, who realised unhappily that she was very near the limit of her endurance. 'Mrs Maitland said I could stay.'

'Of course you're staying.' It had never occurred to him that any other arrangement would be made. 'But wait a minute longer, Clare. There are a couple of things I want to ask you.'

Clare sat down again. To his alarm, she looked immediately hopeful. 'Something that might help you find Harry,' she said.

'Not directly.' But he added, because he couldn't bear to send her to bed without some constructive thought to help her through the long, sleepless hours, 'At least, I gave Inspector Wylie something to think about. Something may come of that.'

'I hope so.' She actually smiled at him then, and he thought again of the eleven-year-old who had clung to him for support in the courtroom, while her whole world came crashing in ruins about her. That wasn't going to happen again if he could help it, but as he smiled back at her he knew in his heart that he believed it was already too late.

'Well, first, after Harry's arrest and the Magistrates' Court hearing, did he ever say anything to you to indicate he thought he was being followed?'

Clare's eye widened as she considered the question. 'I'm sure, if he was, he didn't know it. And we were out together several times, Mr Maitland. I never noticed anybody.'

'You wouldn't, and I don't think Harry did. But it's nice to be sure. Now, did he ever tell you about the people he met at the Mariners' Arms?'

'He told me when he went to South Ealing, of course, he said it was "research". That seemed to be some sort of a joke,' said Clare, wrinkling her forehead over its obscurity. 'As for the people he met there, I met Jim Rickover once.'

'What did you make of him?'

'I didn't think he seemed very important.'

'You know, I think you're right about that.'

'Harry said it was all pretty boring, he had to listen to a lot of technical stuff, because that was the kind of thing they were all interested in, but there was one of them, Julian – I don't remember his other name – who liked the same sort of things that we do. He was a bit more amusing, Harry said.'

'Did he mention Basil Vlasov?'

'Yes, because I thought it was another friend from the Embassy perhaps, and I was surprised when he explained he was the head of the Fenton Laboratory. Harry liked him, I think, but he was curious about him.' At the thought she smiled again, quite spontaneously, and Antony felt a sudden sense of chill; because it was the smile of one who remembers a loved one with affection, but who is no longer troubled by hope. Clare, it seemed, had travelled a long way since that

132

morning. 'But I don't think,' she went on, 'that he got very far with his questions.'

'Just one other thing then, and I won't keep you any longer. Did Harry make a habit of meeting Vladimir at Jenners'?'

'Oh, yes, he always went there. In fact, Harry never goes anywhere else, if it's his choice. He says you get so much better service where you're known.'

'How did he discover the place in the beginning?'

'Vladimir took him there.'

'I see. Did you ever meet him?'

'Yes, I liked him. If there was a plot, Mr Maitland, I don't think he was part of it.

'Don't you indeed?'

'He *liked* England.' There was no doubt that Clare was taking his questions seriously. 'Actually, he made no secret of the fact that he was happier here than in Russia.'

'Thank you. That's all, Clare. I hope you sleep well. But she won't, of course,' he added, after their visitor had gone up the steep stairs that led to the attics, one of which they had made into a reasonably comfortable spare room. 'Has she got everything she needs?'

'Everything except peace of mind,' said Jenny, sighing. 'I'll take her to the studio to pack a bag tomorrow, and I'll talk to her parents, and to Barbara as well, in case they're worried.'

'She thinks Charlton's dead, doesn't she?'

'She hasn't said so, but I'm afraid she does.' Jenny gave that a moment's unhappy consideration. 'And now, Antony, you'd better tell me. What did that man want?'

'To give me some rather unpalatable information, and to ask me about Basil. If I'm going to talk, love, I think I'll have a beer instead of brandy. Can I get one for you too?'

'You may as well.' She waited patiently enough until the tumbler was at her elbow, but her eyes were anxious and as soon as he had seated himself she asked, 'What was the – the unpalatable information, Antony?'

He didn't want to tell her, but there was no help for it. Besides, in the last few days the habit of frankness where she

133

was concerned seemed to have grown on him. 'He says that Briggs thinks – and perhaps other people too – that I may be trying to help Charlton because of my political convictions.'

That took Jenny a moment to assimilate. 'But you don't have any political convictions,' she said at last in a bewildered tone.

'Not that kind, certainly.'

'But . . . it's just ridiculous,' said Jenny severely, as the full force of what he had said hit her. 'I never heard such nonsense in my life.'

'All the same . . . it isn't important, love.'

'I don't think Inspector Wylie can be a very sensible man.'

'It's Briggs's opinion, not his. Or so he says.'

Jenny ignored this. 'And now you say he's asking questions about Basil too.'

'That, he said, was the main purpose of his visit.' Even to Jenny he couldn't bring himself to voice his own doubts. 'But he gave me some information too.'

'If it's more of Superintendent Briggs's slanders – '

'Nothing like that.' He told her as briefly as he could about Harry Charlton's shadows, and the misfortunes that had befallen them. 'I don't believe Harry even knew he was being followed, let alone that he slugged this chap Meredith, and that makes me wonder about Meredith's part in the events of Friday night.'

'You think he might have murdered the witness himself?'

'That, or been a party to it. And if he were involved that would explain some other things too.'

'What things?'

'The planting of the documents, the stealing of Harry's necktie.' He took his glass from where he had placed it on the mantelpiece and went to join her on the sofa. 'I'm going to see Meredith tomorrow, with Wylie sitting in on the interview,' he said. 'But I can't see that it will do the slightest good.'

'You never know. You've often said yourself, Antony, you never know where things may lead. Besides . . . you told us about the people you saw this afternoon, but you didn't say what conclusions you had drawn.'

'Uncle Nick would have accused me of guessing.'

'Then you have got some idea. I thought you had,' said Jenny triumphantly.

'I always have ideas. They don't always work out,' he reminded her. 'And this one is too nebulous even to put into words. There is also the fact that I may be working on a false premise, after all.'

'How do you mean?'

'I was looking for somebody at the laboratory who had some personal knowledge of Harry Charlton – '

'That was my idea,' said Jenny, looking guilty.

' – but it only occurred to me later that perhaps that knowledge had been supplied by his friend, Vladimir.' He paused, and drank some of his beer. 'I don't see my way, love,' he added gloomily.

'You'll have to tell Uncle Nick about what Superintendent Briggs thinks,' said Jenny, in just as depressed a tone.

'I'll make time tomorrow. He won't like it, but I suppose in this instance honesty is the lesser of two evils.' He contemplated that for a moment and then said with more energy, 'Who lives may learn. Do you think you could persuade Vera to ask Clare to dinner tomorrow?'

'I should think so. She knows how fond Uncle Nick is of her, and nobody could say Vera isn't a kind person. But – '

'We'll eat out for a change, Jenny. I thought I'd take you to Jenners',' he told her. And couldn't be persuaded to give any better reason than, 'If you remember, the food's very good,' no matter how persuasively she asked him.

It wasn't until they were in bed that she remembered to tell him, 'Roger phoned.'

'I thought they were still in Grunning's Hole.'

'So did I, but they got back this afternoon. Meg starts rehearsals of her new play tomorrow. And I asked them to come in the evening, so if we're going out we'll have to let them know.'

'We'll take them with us.' No use explaining to Jenny at this stage that if he'd known Roger was available . . .

But perhaps she guessed his thought, though she said only, sleepily, 'Too late, Antony, too late,' and did not attempt to question him further about his intentions.

Oddly enough, they both slept well that night; though the thing that was on Antony's mind when he awoke next morning wasn't Harry Charlton's plight, or Clare's distress, or even his own dilemma, but the talk he had promised Jenny he would have some time during the day with Uncle Nick.

MONDAY, 18th OCTOBER

I

The first job that morning was to talk to Mr Bellerby, which he didn't at all enjoy, and after he had explained matters briefly to try to avoid the suggestion of a meeting, Antony was aware of a feeling of regret as he replaced the receiver; the solicitor was a kindly man, and had besides his share of human curiosity. But tomorrow was also a good day.

Even then he didn't hurry himself, having already arranged not to go in to chambers, and having decided for some reason that the time of the coffee break would be most suitable for interviewing the elusive Mrs Edwards. But when he came out of the station at South Ealing into a morning that was crisp and pleasantly bright, he found he had still a good half hour in hand before the deadline he had set himself was reached. Basil had told him that all the people he was interested in lived close to the laboratory; if his sense of direction didn't fail him, he thought he could place himself in that general area, and then ask his way. In any case there was, this morning, no sign of a taxi. He set out to walk.

As he went he tried to put his thoughts in order. Yesterday had been illuminating, in more ways than one, but now that he came to consider the matter he began to realise that perhaps asking to interview the Special Branch man, Meredith, hadn't been the wisest thing he could have done. It all depended, really, on how much Wylie believed of this preposterous theory of Briggs's. If he didn't believe it, even if he had any serious doubts about its truth, it might have been possible to persuade him of the validity of the accusation. And once that was done, Wylie had facilities – which a mere member of the bar did not – to launch a full-scale investigation.

Even Uncle Nick couldn't object to that course of action. But it would be slow, so damnably slow. If Harry Charlton were still alive . . .

All the same, when he came to a telephone box he found change, found the tattered envelope on which he had inscribed Wylie's number, and put through a call. But it was no use, the man wasn't at his desk, and no one seemed to know where he might be reached.

By his reckoning, he was now in the same general area that he had visited yesterday, and he decided that the time had come to ask his way. Against all precedent, the first person he approached turned out to be a local man, very willing to help. The Fenton Laboratory was in the next street. 'Turn left when you get there, and it's on the right, about half a mile further on.' Antony thanked him and proceeded on his way.

It was a modern, one-storey building, nothing fancy; which he might have guessed, he supposed, from what Basil had had to say about its beginnings. Security seemed to be well maintained; Basil had left instructions for his admission, but he was escorted to his office, presumably lest curiosity should lead him into any prohibited part of the premises. Then the guard waited with him while Mr Vlasov was summoned. The office was an austere little room, and from the bareness of the desk it didn't look as if its owner spent much time there.

Basil arrived, after an interval, with a pleasant-looking woman of about thirty-five in tow. 'Vince told me you jumped the gun and saw him and Julian yesterday, so I thought it must be Sheila you wanted to see this morning. Antony Maitland, an old friend of mine, Sheila. I told you, he's Harry Charlton's counsel.' He waved an invitation – the chairs were modern, but not uncomfortable – and went to seat himself behind the desk. 'Do you want me to go?' he asked, looking very much as though it would take an explosion to shift him.

'No, of course not.' So Basil wasn't altogether lacking in inquisitiveness. Somehow the thought was a consoling one.

'That's good. They're bringing us some coffee . . . here it is now.'

So far Sheila Edwards had said nothing, though she had acknowledged Basil's introduction with a rather forced smile. Now, while the coffee was poured, Antony took the opportunity of studying her. A resolute-looking woman, not very tall, with square shoulders and a determinedly tweedy look. And his first impression had been that she had a pleasant face, but now, watching her, he began to wonder uneasily whether there was going to be much pleasantness about their coming talk. Sure enough, as soon as the three of them were alone together, she said bluntly, 'In spite of Basil's explanations I don't altogether understand your purpose in coming here. Surely Charlton's arrest ended the matter, once and for all.'

'As far as I was concerned, that was the beginning,' Maitland pointed out.

'That seems to be no reason why you should try to involve the rest of us.'

'Do you object to answering my questions, Mrs Edwards?'

She thought about that. 'Yes, I think I do,' she said at last.

'In that case – ' He glanced at Basil, who was sipping coffee and looking sphinx-like; once more the familiar friend he had been on Saturday evening, not the stranger he had somehow become in the intervening period. He became aware that Sheila Edwards was still speaking.

'However, as a favour to Basil,' she was saying, 'and provided you understand I shall refuse to answer anything I consider impertinent – '

Maitland did not allow her time to finish before he was taking her up on the offer. 'What did you think of Harry Charlton?' he asked.

For the first time her lips quivered in something approaching a smile. 'I used the word just now . . . impertinent,' she said. 'Needless to say, he didn't get any information out of me. The other thing was, it was really rather tedious having him tagging along like that. He used to get into the most boring conversations with Julian.'

'How soon did you suspect what he was after?'

'As soon as I knew his occupation, whenever that was.'

'You put it down to professional curiosity, then, nothing more sinister?'

'Why, yes, I suppose I did.' She hesitated. 'Vince was the only one of us who treated it seriously, but I don't think even he had any idea of Charlton meaning to pass over information to the enemy. You didn't, did you, Basil?'

'It never occurred to me,' said Vlasov shortly. 'But I explained that to you, Antony, on Saturday night.'

'So you did. I take it then, Mrs Edwards, that of your group it was Mr Shacklock who got on best with Harry Charlton.'

'If you except Jim Rickover. They were more of an age. But Julian wasn't above pulling his leg, fake technical stuff, you know. We all played up with that, except Vince.' She stopped there, but leaving him with the impression that she had more to say, so he waited patiently while she looked in rather a searching way from him to Basil and then back to him again. 'You're trying to find a scapegoat,' she said then. 'Someone with more knowledge of the project than Jim had. I suppose Basil told you which of us to concentrate on.'

It was no part of his desire to stir up trouble between Basil and his staff. 'I outlined my specifications, and he told me who would fit them,' said Maitland cautiously. 'You see, it soon became obvious that Rickover wasn't the best source of the sort of information an enemy agent would need.'

'No, but Charlton hadn't the sense to know that.'

To argue would merely be to exacerbate her further. And he had got what he came for – hadn't he? – the same thing he had got out of yesterday's interviews, a sight of someone he regarded as suspect. 'Would you be willing to postulate for a moment that Harry Charlton might be innocent?' he asked, in an oddly tentative way.

'What would follow if I did?'

'Some questions about your colleagues.'

'You saw Vince and Julian yesterday, Vince tells me. Did they talk about me?'

He smiled at that, ruefully. 'Only to tell me you were unlikely to be at home on a fine Sunday afternoon.'

Again she considered for a moment, perhaps she was deciding whether or not that might be regarded as actionable. Then she got to her feet. 'And Basil?' she said.

'Basil's unhelpfulness' – Maitland began to move towards the door as he spoke – 'was the reason I had to see you all. He insisted that all his friends were above suspicion.'

'Thank you for nothing.' That was addressed to Basil with a distinctly hostile look. 'And have you come to any conclusion?' she added, turning back to Antony.

'No firm conclusion,' he told her. Let her make what she liked out of that.

'Hardly worth coming, was it?'

'On the contrary.' He couldn't resist what he hoped was an enigmatic expression. The lady was beginning to annoy him. She held his eyes for a moment longer and then, as he held the door open for her, swept past him without another word.

Vlasov sank back in his chair as Maitland crossed the room towards the desk again. 'If that was all you wanted,' he said reproachfully, 'was there any real purpose served by alienating my staff?'

'Have I alienated . . . Shacklock and Brewer, for instance?'

'They seem to have taken your questions reasonably well. But Sheila isn't normally a prickly person, you know.'

'Isn't she? I only know she didn't like me, you might say she came in here determined not to. And nothing I could have said or done would have made things any better . . . or worse.'

'I can't see what you got out of it. And what did you mean, "no firm conclusion"?' asked Basil querulously.

'Exactly what I said, neither more nor less.'

Basil gave him an odd look. 'You're not telling me the truth,' he complained. 'I think you've made up your mind, though heaven knows on what evidence – '

Maitland ignored that. 'How far is this project of yours from completion?' he asked.

'Who can say? Six days, six weeks.'

'Let's put it another way. Would it be worth anybody's

while to – to defect, let us say, with the information as it now stands?'

'Antony, are you seriously telling me – ?'

'I was never more serious in my life.'

'Well then, I can only tell you what I should do if I were the person concerned. I'd wait until the job was finished and go over in a blaze of glory. On the other hand, if some emergency arose, if I thought I was going to be found out for instance, I'd cut my losses. That's obvious.'

'I'm afraid it is. May I give you some advice, Basil? Shut up shop, send everybody home – '

'Now? Today?'

'Exactly. And get the security people to make damn sure nobody takes anything out with them. I take it there's no question of the whole thing being carried in somebody's head?'

'No, that isn't possible.' Basil sounded stunned. 'But I can't do that,' he went on, as the full implications of what Antony had said came home to him. 'I can't tell my people I don't trust them.'

'Don't tell them anything.'

'But it would be obvious. Anyway, how long – ?'

'I can't give you the answer to that.'

'It can't be done,' said Basil flatly.

'It was only a suggestion.' But it had been more than that, it had been a hope – the only one he had – that some at least of the urgency might be removed from the situation.

'If you told me who – '

'Without definite proof, would you be prepared to take my word for it? That might only be to make matters worse,' said Antony. All this time he had been standing, looking down at his friend, but now he turned away, moving stiffly as though he were very tired. 'I'll do what I can,' he added.

Basil came quickly round the desk and reached the door before him. 'What, for instance?' he demanded.

'Well, first, talk to a chap called Wylie, whom I think you know. If I don't get anywhere with him . . . I can't tell you, Basil, I don't know.' He paused, and then went on with a

142

smile, 'I have to go, and I can't while you're guarding the door like that.'

Vlasov moved, but he seemed to do so with reluctance. 'I can't say you've done anything to set my mind at rest,' he grumbled, following Maitland out into the hallway.

'I know. I'm sorry. But that wasn't the object of the exercise, you know,' said Antony gently.

II

There was a glass-paned door, and then a concrete path about five yards long leading to the gate in the heavy, wire enclosure. Antony stepped out into the sunshine, had a polite word with the man who let him out, and began to walk back along the pavement the way he had come, beside the tall, wire fence. Since he left home that morning the thought of the possible 'reaction' he had mentioned so glibly to Jenny had never been far from his thoughts. But now, intent on the implications of his talk with Sheila Edwards and his later brief exchange with Basil, all idea of possible danger had passed from his mind. It wasn't until he had been walking for nearly five minutes that he realised he was being followed.

It was a wide street, but the traffic, both motorised and pedestrian, was heavy. It wasn't easy to be sure, so many people were going in the same direction, and at first he discounted the impression, dismissing it almost angrily as the result of a mixture of cowardice and imagination. But somebody's footsteps were keeping pace with his own, and after a moment he acknowledged to himself ruefully that the sixth sense acquired so painfully so many years ago wasn't likely to be deceiving him. The thing was, what next?

He wasn't left long in doubt. Later, when he was trying to explain how he knew what was going on, he found himself at a loss for words; but then, thinking of Vera, it occurred to

143

him that perhaps the best analogy would be to a composer, hearing clearly in his head all the different strains of his orchestral arrangement; in much the same way he himself could concentrate on one man, with what seemed to him a distinctive way of walking, and gradually he became aware that the footsteps were drawing closer.

They were approaching a traffic light, which changed to red just as he was about to step onto the crossing. Not a good place to be, on the very edge of the pavement with the traffic pouring past, a car, two buses, another car, a heavy articulated lorry. It was as the lorry was hurtling towards him that he felt it, as he would certainly never have done if he hadn't already been on the alert, the merest touch on his shoulder, hardly more than a brushing against his jacket. He swept round suddenly, his left hand coming up automatically to grip the wrist of the man who stood behind him; a heavily-built man with horn-rimmed glasses and a round, guileless face.

For a moment they stood there, eyes locked, while the lorry thundered past. Then the stranger looked down pointedly. 'If I touched you in the crowd, I'm sorry,' he said mildly. 'But aren't you over-reacting?'

Antony let him go. The lights changed again and the flock of pedestrians streamed past him, jostling him as they went but there was no menace now. 'If you want to earn your pay, you'll have to do better than that,' he said.

The stranger's expression was politely bewildered. 'I haven't the faintest idea what you're talking about,' he said, and turned away, walking quickly back the way they had come.

Maitland made his way home without further incident. He was preoccupied mainly with the thought that his idea had been proved right . . . somebody wanted to put him out of the way of making further enquiries, at least for the time being. Even so, the reaction from the brush with danger, brief though it had been, a feeling of excitement that was almost exhilaration, lasted him throughout the journey, and it was only when he let himself into the hall and found Gibbs hovering near the study door that the reverse side of the affair presented itself to him. He was sure now in his own mind that he was on the right track, but what use was that when nobody would believe him?

III

The first thing he did when he got upstairs was to telephone Wylie again, this time successfully. 'I suppose it's too late to stop you setting up that interview with Meredith,' he said without preamble, as soon as he was put through.

'Having second thoughts, Mr Maitland?' There was a smug sound about that; well, he hadn't expected anything else.

'Not in the way you mean. It's just that I've thought of a better way of dealing with the matter.'

'Then you're in luck. Meredith isn't back on duty again yet, but he isn't at home and no one seems to know where to get in touch with him.'

It occurred to Antony that this was probably rather an odd state of affairs, even granting that Meredith was still on sick leave, but to stress his doubts at the moment might only be to put Wylie's back up. He remarked instead, 'I'm still hoping to see you, Inspector.'

'Now, why should that be, I wonder?'

'There are things I should tell you.'

'Such as?'

He was about to answer that when he heard the door, and turned to see Jenny follow Clare into the room. 'Nothing I can go into over the phone,' he said. 'But it is important.'

'Something that has happened since last night,' said Wylie reflectively. 'Very well, Mr Maitland, where shall we meet?'

'If you could add to your kindness by coming to chambers – ' That sounded unduly formal, but he wanted Wylie's co-operation, and one false step and it would be all up with that. Surprisingly, though, the suggestion was accepted without demur.

'Three o'clock, then,' said Wylie briskly, and rang off without even having to ask for the address.

Clare was wearing a clean blouse, so presumably the expedition to the studio had taken place that morning. She still appeared subdued and he had the feeling that Jenny's customary air of serenity was hardly held – probably her talk with the Cannings had something to do with that – but this was no time to comment on either fact. He hadn't reckoned, however, on the reverse being true . . . if he could observe them, they both had their own reasons for analysing his looks. Jenny said nothing, but Clare asked eagerly:

'Has something happened?'

He thought perhaps, in his present, uncharacteristic need for reassurance, he would have confided in Jenny even the attempt on his life, but the information could do nothing to set Clare's fears at rest. 'Nothing I can prove,' he said. And then, seeking as he had done the night before for some words of encouragement, 'But if I can persuade Inspector Wylie to take some action – '

'He might be able to get the proof,' said Jenny, as matter-of-factly as if she were saying it was a fine day. But when he turned to her, saying enthusiastically, 'That's it exactly, love,' she shook her head at him and added with a half smile, 'You got your reaction, Antony, didn't you?' so that he forgot about Clare and her problems for the moment in the more pressing need to hearten her.

'A very feeble reaction . . . amateurish,' he told her.

Clare looked from one of them to the other. 'I don't understand,' she said. And when neither of them made any immediate move to enlighten her went on sadly, 'It isn't enough to clear Harry of the charges against him, now, when we don't know where he is.'

Explain to her that there was nothing he could do – one man working alone – that the police and the Special Branch couldn't do a hundred times as well? Explain to her that in everything he did he was relying on instinct, of which he had a profound distrust? 'Trust me, Clare,' he said, and knew as she turned to him saying, with all the affectionate generosity of her nature, 'Oh, I do, I do,' that this was perhaps the worst reproach of all. She did trust him, and Harry Charlton had trusted him, and over the most important point of all he was almost certain now that he was going to let them down.

IV

He left again for the Inner Temple as soon as lunch was over. Sir Nicholas, Jenny had told him, hadn't been home for the meal, and if he had eaten alone that wouldn't be likely to have taken him very long. Sure enough, his uncle was already back in his room when Antony arrived in chambers. He was working on a brief, old Mr Mallory told him, obviously with the intention of discouraging any interruption of this very necessary activity; more welcome news was that Sir Nicholas had no appointments until four o'clock.

This was as he had hoped, so there was no reason, Maitland told himself, for the slight but definite sinking of his spirits that the information brought about. He tapped lightly on the door, awaited his uncle's summons, and went into the big, familiar room. Sir Nicholas removed his spectacles, placed them carefully on top of the document he had been perusing, and sat back more comfortably in his chair as though preparing himself for a long session.

'Ah, Antony,' he said. 'I was hoping for a word with you.'

'If you have time, Uncle Nick.'

'I think in the circumstances,' said Sir Nicholas reflectively, 'I should make time whatever my other commitments. Gibbs tells me that Inspector Wylie spent some time with you yesterday evening.'

'Yes, he did. Our talk was not unilluminating.'

'That is gratifying, of course. Is his attitude towards you as hostile as that of Chief Superintendent Briggs, I wonder?'

'I honestly don't know. Not openly so, at any rate.' He hesitated, but anything would be better, after all, than being treated with this sort of gentle politeness, when he knew perfectly well his uncle was as mad as fire. 'He told me Briggs has persuaded himself I'm a communist, and that's my link with Harry Charlton,' Maitland said deliberately. 'I couldn't gather how widespread the view is, or whether Wylie himself shares it.'

Sir Nicholas's lips tightened, but that was the only outward sign he gave that he found the news unpalatable. Antony, who could have coped with a slanging match, felt his spirits sink still further. 'This is really too much,' said his uncle quietly after a moment. Maitland ventured a cautious agreement.

'That's what I thought, sir.' And suddenly the older man smiled at him.

'It has occurred to me, Antony, that our disagreements on this subject have gone far enough. Besides this – this aberration of the Chief Superintendent's is too foolish to be taken seriously. Even your dealings with him – which I have had occasion in the past to point out were not always wise – cannot altogether excuse so bizarre an idea.'

Maitland was still trying to adjust himself to this complete reversal of everything he had expected. He came round the desk now and sank into the leather chair at the other side of the fire. Sir Nicholas swivelled his own chair round to face him. 'You are not going to tell me,' he said, gently mocking, 'that you thought I should subscribe to this nonsense.'

'I thought you'd say the whole thing was my own fault,' said Antony bluntly.

'It is a temptation, of course.' Sir Nicholas's tone was pensive. 'There have been so many occasions in the past . . . but we agreed, did we not, that in this instance at least you must be held blameless? The question therefore arises, what have your further researches revealed? If I know you, you did not come away empty-handed from your talk with Inspector Wylie.'

'I wanted to tell you about that,' said Maitland, still bewildered by this change of front, 'but I wasn't so sure you'd be willing to listen.'

148

'I am, above all, a reasonable man,' said Sir Nicholas, which was so blatantly untrue that his nephew was betrayed into grinning at him. 'As a member of chambers, I hope I should always display an interest in your activities on behalf of a client.'

'Even in my meddling beyond the call of duty in the affairs of a chap you believe to be guilty?'

But even this continued outspokenness – not wise, perhaps, but irresistible – did not provoke Sir Nicholas. He only smiled again in an unnervingly saintly way and said mildly, 'I am sure you are going to attempt to change my mind about that, my dear boy.'

'Well, I am. And you're quite right, I did get something out of my talk with Wylie . . . the answer to a question that had been troubling me ever since Foster's murder.'

'And what was that?'

'When Charlton appeared in the Magistrates' Court no opposition was made to bail. I could see only one reason for that, they hoped he would lead them to his associate or associates. Jim Rickover – I don't know whether I made this clear to you, Uncle Nick – hadn't sufficient knowledge of the project concerned to make a very convincing ally for someone seriously engaged in obtaining information for the enemy.'

'So if Charlton was being followed, where was the man who was doing the following while Foster was being killed?'

'Exactly. The answer is, he turned up in hospital next morning, saying he'd been hit over the head . . . that must have been well before nine o'clock, but he wasn't found until close on midnight. When he recovered consciousness he couldn't remember who he was or what he had been doing, but later his memory came back. So I wondered – '

'There may have been a good reason for his not having been found before.'

'He was in a mews . . . non-residential, just six garages. Nobody bothered to find out whether any of the tenants had been in or out during the crucial time.'

'If they trusted him, there was no reason why they should.'

'I suppose not. All the same – '

'All the same, I think you are building too much on a very slight indication.'

Maitland didn't bother to point out that he hadn't explained his conclusions, he was too used to his uncle's mind marching with his own. 'Wait a bit,' he said. 'I told you his memory came back. The thing is, he remembered too much.'

'I'm beginning to see.'

'I thought you might. He remembered everything that had happened, up to and including the blow on the head. And you know as well as I do, Uncle Nick – Dr Macintosh explained it to us when there was that business of Peter losing his memory – that's just not possible.'

'Retrograde amnesia.' Trust Uncle Nick to have that tucked away in his memory somewhere. 'Have you confided your suspicions to Inspector Wylie?'

'Well, I did, but without mentioning that really clinching point. I thought I'd like to spring it on the man – his name's Meredith – myself. But luckily Wylie couldn't get hold of him this morning, because now I think it will be better to talk to him instead . . . to Wylie, I mean. If he can be persuaded to take the matter up, from the point of view of Charlton's innocence – '

'I have to point out to you, Antony, that Meredith's possible complicity is no sort of proof of that.' He paused, and gave his nephew one of his more searching looks. 'There's more to it than that, isn't there?'

'The identity of the senior member of the staff at the laboratory, who I think was the source of the leakage of information. And that doesn't prove Charlton's innocence either,' Maitland added rather desperately. 'But when you take into consideration the fact that it means the case against him was deliberately manufactured, I think it creates a strong presumption in his favour.'

'That sounds well, but there's a fallacy there somewhere,' said Sir Nicholas, frowning over the problem. 'It doesn't matter who gave him the information, if the rest of the things alleged against him are true.'

Antony thought about that. 'Thank you for setting me straight,' he said after a moment.

'Come now, you can't tell me you're really grateful.'

'No, really, Uncle Nick. I admit the whole affair's got me confused, but it's no use blinking the facts. In any case, if I can get Wylie moving at all it should be sufficient. You see, I believe that any trail he finds will lead away from Harry Charlton.'

'You are hopeful then of clearing him of the charges that have been laid against him, and of the charge of murder that would certainly have been laid had he not disappeared.'

'I wouldn't say exactly hopeful. And I know you're thinking that isn't much good when we don't know where he is. But, you see, there's the question of Basil's project. If nothing is done, the details will go to the Russians in due course, while the authorities are congratulating themselves that their action against Charlton nipped the whole thing in the bud.'

'If you could be induced to use expressions that are a little less trite – ' But Sir Nicholas was on his best behaviour this afternoon, he did not pursue the complaint. 'I see what you mean, of course,' he went on reflectively. And then, with what neither he nor his nephew regarded as a change of subject, 'How is Clare today?'

'Subdued.' He considered the word and found it satisfactory. 'Poor child, she's afraid I think her ungrateful. Ungrateful . . . as if I'd accomplished anything! So she chattered all through lunch, trying to prove how confident she is, while all the time she's quite sure Harry is dead. Uncle Nick, it's heartbreaking!'

Sir Nicholas, who had been toying with his pencil, looked up at that, and for a long moment his eyes met his nephew's. And suddenly Antony was on the defensive again. 'I know what you're thinking, Uncle Nick. I've hurt Jenny over and over again, right from the beginning when she was younger than Clare is now.'

'I was thinking of Jenny, certainly, and of you. But not

151

quite in the way you mean.' He did not attempt to expand on that statement, but got up to attend to the fire, choosing each piece of fuel with as much care as if the achievement of symmetry was the most important thing in the world. 'You must not think me unsympathetic with what you are trying to do for Clare,' he went on, when matters were arranged to his liking. 'Only until I can accept your premise of Charlton's innocence I cannot agree that you are going the best way about helping her.'

Antony had nothing to say to that. He watched in silence while his uncle seated himself again, and repressed his own instinct to get up and move about the room. 'There would be one very positive advantage to proving Charlton's innocence,' said Sir Nicholas, after the silence had lengthened a little. 'Chief Superintendent Briggs could hardly persist in this idea he has got into his head about you.'

'No, he couldn't, could he?' Maitland sounded almost uninterested. He thought the truce was on again, but he wasn't quite sure. 'Look here, sir, can I tell you my conclusions about the real source of the leak at the laboratory?'

'I have been waiting for half an hour for you to do so,' said Sir Nicholas, with something of his usual tartness. This time Antony did get to his feet.

'You know the people I was concentrating on, and you know the reason,' he began.

'I know their names. And I gathered – more from what you didn't say than from anything you told us – that after your interviews on Sunday you felt obliged to add the name of your friend Vlasov to the list.'

'Yes, well, it gave me a shock when his name came up and I couldn't help wondering . . . but it won't wash, Uncle Nick.' Sir Nicholas might have been observed to raise his eyes despairingly to heaven. 'If Basil had wanted to return to the home of his fathers he could have taken his idea with him years ago, and done all the work on the other side.'

'That seems a logical argument.'

Antony took a quick turn to the window and back again.

This scene had been played so often, he should have felt completely at home in his role as special pleader, but the mood of unease persisted. 'I have to admit to a fault in the reasoning that led me to concentrate on the people who knew Harry Charlton from meeting him at the Mariners' Arms,' he said, 'but I think I have reached the right conclusion for all that, so perhaps it doesn't matter.'

'You will forgive me for reserving judgment.'

'It's what I expected. I have three points to make in vindication of my views.' (This was going to be awkward.) 'And I may as well tell you straight away, you're not going to like one of them.'

That brought another rather searching look from his uncle, but Sir Nicholas said only, 'That does not surprise me. But you're beginning at the wrong end, Antony. What is your opinion?'

Maitland turned away. He was looking into the fire as he spoke. 'I think the source of the leak is Basil's second-in-command, Vincent Brewer.'

'I thought you told me he was a true-blue Tory.'

'No doubt he was once. But he was married a few years ago to a woman with very decided left-wing views, with whom he is very much in love. I can't quite describe the feeling those two gave me, Uncle Nick, as if they were one person. Ostensibly they disagree about politics, but she is very much the dominant personality and I think he would be willing to go along with anything she suggested.'

'That's all very well, but not all radicals – '

'I know. Three points, Uncle Nick. May I make them?'

'Certainly you may.' At his tone, Maitland glanced round at him again, but there was nothing to be told from the older man's expression but a general impression of courteous interest.

'The first point has to do with character, and I admit – not having seen Mrs Edwards at home – the distinction may not apply in her case. The Brewers struck me as a completely humourless couple, extremely serious-minded about their

153

pleasures. Translation to a Moscow suburb might not seem too great a hardship to them. But I cannot, on any account, see Julian Shacklock giving up his present, sybaritic life-style.'

'You have considered the possibility, of course, that the traitor – I do not think that is too strong a word – does not intend to defect.'

'I don't think he'd have any choice. If the complete plans . . . formula . . . whatever . . . reach the other side, that fact will become known. At which point it will be perfectly obvious that Jim Rickover was not the source of the information, and the kind of investigation that would ensue . . . they wouldn't risk it.'

'That's a good point, certainly, but you have still to demonstrate to me that Harry Charlton is innocent, that anyone else is involved.'

'I'm coming to that. But there is still the matter of the attitude of my three suspects to my enquiries. Both Shacklock and Mrs Edwards showed, in their own vastly differing ways, some awareness of the implications of my questions. Sheila Edwards resented them, which was reasonable enough; Shacklock didn't, but he made it quite clear he knew what I was up to. Whereas neither of the Brewers showed by word or look that they thought there was any special significance behind my visit.' He paused a moment, and now his eyes were searching his uncle's face anxiously. 'Do you think that was natural?' he demanded.

'Given your premise, the inference you have drawn seems a reasonable one,' said Sir Nicholas cautiously.

'I suppose' – Maitland's tone was bitter – 'that's as cordial an agreement as I have a right to expect.' He moved away from the fire, went again to the window and back. 'The next point may strike you more forcibly,' he said, coming again to a halt at the corner of the desk. 'Harry Charlton's disappearance ought to have put a stop to my interest in the affair . . . my extraordinary interest, anyway. So I knew if there was any reaction to my continued enquiries it would mean that I was on the right track.'

That was more than Sir Nicholas could be expected to bear without protest. 'I am not quite sure what you mean by reaction – ' he began.

'I think you know very well.' Antony did not wait for him to finish. 'You've given me enough warnings of what might happen. Well, the reaction came all right. Somebody tried to shove me under a bus this morning.'

He wasn't quite sure what response he had expected to this statement. With Uncle Nick you never knew which way the cat would jump. What he got was a stony look and a coldly spoken question. 'In view of this does it come as a surprise to you, Antony, that I disapprove of your meddling in an affair of this nature?'

Maitland essayed a smile. He had the feeling it didn't go down well. 'I believe you have made me tolerably familiar with your views,' he said dryly.

Surprisingly, this piece of deliberate provocation aroused a sympathetic response. At least, that was how Antony chose to interpret it. 'There can be no profit, then, in further examining my feelings,' said Sir Nicholas. 'I think, however, that you had better tell me exactly what happened.'

'Nothing much. Really, Uncle Nick! I should have said a lorry, not a bus, and the chap never actually got as far as pushing me. I got the feeling I was being followed, you see, after I left the laboratory.'

'Your unfortunate past,' murmured Sir Nicholas, who had been known to refer to 'that bunch of thugs in Whitehall' during his nephew's wartime service.

'Yes, well, it's a sort of sixth sense, I suppose, something you don't lose with the years. Anyway, he came up behind me, but I turned and grabbed his wrist before he had chance to do more than touch me. We exchanged a few words, and he made off the way we had come.'

Sir Nicholas was giving what seemed to be undue care to the straightening out of a paper clip, but now he looked up from his task. 'Antony, are you sure?' he asked.

155

'Quite sure.' He resisted the temptation to elaborate on that, and after a moment his uncle spoke again.

'This changes things rather,' he said reflectively. 'But you were going to tell me the conclusions you have drawn from this rather distressing fact.'

'I phoned Basil while I was at home at lunch time to ask him if he'd told Sheila Edwards that I was visiting the lab this morning. He said he hadn't. When I left Shacklock's place – he was the first one I visited, if you remember – I didn't know I shouldn't find her at home. But by the time I got to the Brewers' I had already called at the Edwardses' house, and I mentioned specifically to Brewer that it meant I should have to go out to South Ealing again this morning. It isn't fool-proof, Uncle Nick, I know that, but it's another and perhaps a stronger indication – '

'Yes, I think so.' Sir Nicholas spoke slowly, and held up his hand for silence when his nephew seemed about to add something to his last statement. 'This Inspector Wylie of yours,' he went on after a pause that was quite long enough to set Maitland fidgeting. 'Would you say he had a trusting disposition?'

Antony went back to his chair. 'Far from it,' he said despondently.

'Have you made any arrangement to see him?'

'He's coming here at three o'clock. Ten minutes from now,' he added, glancing at his watch.

'Then I think, I really think, my dear boy, it will be best if I sit in on your discussion. Perhaps with our joint efforts we may be able to persuade him that there is a case for further investigation.'

Maitland was staring at him. 'But you don't believe me yourself,' he said abruptly.

Sir Nicholas gave him a sudden, companionable smile, though Antony's mood was such that he saw in it something of the sinister. 'Let us say that this last revelation has shaken my faith in my own infallibility,' he said smoothly. 'But there

156

is one further question I should like to ask in the time remaining to us. Vera tells me we are to entertain Clare this evening. What's all this about a dinner-party at Jenners'?'

V

A little over four hours later Antony and Jenny met the Farrells, as arranged, at Jenners' Restaurant. Meg, who was better known to the theatre-going public as Margaret Hamilton, had been a friend of the Maitlands ever since she first came to London to play the role of Lady Macbeth opposite that celebrated but eccentric actor, Joseph Dowling, and she had changed, Antony sometimes thought, surprisingly little in the meantime. True, she had attained an elegance that she had not possessed in the early years, but under it all there was the same forthright nature, not always hidden from her friends.

To an outsider it might have seemed natural that Roger, on his marriage, should have been accepted simply as Meg's husband, but the fact was that both Antony and Jenny valued him for himself. Very early in their acquaintance, circumstances had placed Antony, who wouldn't bear any reference to his injured shoulder either by himself or by anybody else, in a position where he had to rely on Roger's help. After that, imperceptibly and perhaps unexpectedly, confidences came more easily. Roger, who was a member of the Stock Exchange, was a sturdily-built man with an incongruously piratical air about him, and Jenny had been known to remark that he reminded her of the man who 'never went into a room without ejaculating "boom" '; but he had in him a surprising streak of the sensitive, and so far in his dealings with his undeniably temperamental friend, had managed never to put a foot wrong.

Antony and Jenny had been to the restaurant, which was within easy walking distance of Kempenfeldt Square, once before. Meg, after the first greetings, was displaying a simple interest in her surroundings. 'A very masculine place, darling, all that panelling, all this dark leather; I can't think what

157

Jenny and I are doing here.' They were sitting in the lounge until their table in the dining-room was ready, and a waiter was hovering solicitously.

Roger, sensing Antony's impatience to be alone with them, said briskly, 'Never mind the décor, Meg. What do you want to drink?'

'But you know, darling. Dubonnet,' said Meg, with a ravishing smile at the waiter, who reeled visibly but managed to collect himself sufficiently to take the rest of their orders.

'Did you enjoy your holiday?' asked Jenny when they were alone again. She was, in her own way, as impatient as her husband, but more concerned not to show it.

'Heavenly,' said Meg. Roger was almost equally brief.

'It was good,' he said. 'Well, we'd waited long enough for it. And now – '

'But, darling, Ossy needed me,' Meg protested. 'You must see we had to come home.' And Roger, who had taken astonishingly calmly to being Margaret Hamilton's husband, smiled and said confidingly to Jenny:

'It was the part, you see. She couldn't resist it.'

'Well, as to that, and to be perfectly honest with you,' said Meg, 'it doesn't seem to speak as well as it reads. But that's after one day's rehearsal,' she added more cheerfully. 'It may improve on acquaintance.' She picked up her glass and eyed Antony over the rim. 'And now, darling, what's up? You didn't bring us here to talk about the weather.'

Antony gave Roger a look, half amused, half despairing. 'I might have known you'd guess there was something in the wind,' he said. 'It's a long story, though.'

'Which might very well have been told at home. Why here?' Meg demanded, looking round the room.

'It's all right, there's no one within earshot. Why do you think I chose this table?' Antony asked her. 'As for the reason I wanted to come here, I'll tell you that in a moment.'

'First things first,' Roger agreed. 'Behave yourself, Meg, and listen.' Meg took a gulp of her wine, which had arrived with the other drinks so unobtrusively they had hardly noticed, put down the glass, and folded her hands in her lap. 'All right, Antony, the floor is yours.'

'I'd better begin at the beginning.' And that was six days ago, and everything so comparatively simple at that stage he could now hardly remember his own state of mind. But he was used to presenting his facts, and had thought about this business so much he could probably have described it in his sleep. He told them it all: the original charge against Harry Charlton; Clare's involvement ('these young things,' said Meg, sighing); the first murder; Charlton's disappearance and the killing of the detective constable; Briggs's eruption into the peace of Sunday morning and the accusations he had made; and everything that had happened since then, including his brush with the unknown man in the street near the Fenton Laboratory. Jenny had heard that part of the story while they were changing to come out; she made no comment at its repetition, but Roger noticed her hand gripping the stem of her wine-glass until the knuckles were white. And because it was so much on his mind, Antony also made very clear to them his uncle's disapproval of his activities, until this afternoon, when he had shown some signs of relenting.

'If he was willing to sit in on your talk with Wylie – ' said Roger thoughtfully. Maitland did not allow him time to take the idea any further.

'He doesn't want a scandal, any more than I do. If Harry's cleared, I'm cleared of these rumours about my political affiliations.'

That was too much for Jenny. 'You're not being fair, Antony. Uncle Nick is concerned for you, that's all.'

'You may be right.' He sounded almost uninterested in the subject, but none of them was deceived by that. It was in the forefront of his mind, and they knew it.

'This chap Wylie,' said Roger. 'He at least must know perfectly well that Briggs's theory is all nonsense.'

'Not necessarily. Plenty of people don't show their true colours until the crunch comes. It doesn't matter, anyway. The important thing is that Wylie came. And Uncle Nick did more than sit in on the interview, he made all my points for me, just as though he believed them himself. You know how impressive he can be. It would have taken a braver man than Wylie to refuse to undertake a course of action that he made appear so eminently reasonable.'

'You're going too fast, darling,' said Meg. 'What exactly was it that Inspector Wylie agreed to?'

'To set in motion a full enquiry from my point of view. That means investigating the Brewers, and Meredith, and the possibility that Harry Charlton was kidnapped.'

'But that's good, isn't it?'

'Of course it's good. Mind you, I'm not saying Wylie believes all my theories, but at least he'll give them a chance.'

'Inspector Sykes always says if you know where to look it's surprising what you find,' said Jenny.

'Chief Inspector,' Antony corrected her automatically. 'It's quite true, only unfortunately in this case, even if he's successful, it doesn't go far enough.'

'If he's successful it would get you off the hook,' Roger reminded him.

'Don't think I'm not aware of the fact. The trouble is, there's Harry Charlton to consider . . . if he's alive. And Clare.'

That brought a moment's silence. 'Which brings us back to the question Meg asked you in the beginning,' said Roger at last. 'Why did you particularly want to come here this evening?'

'Uncle Nick asked me that too. And I couldn't give him any logical reason, except to say that the name kept cropping up. You all know I don't go much for instinct' – he took a moment to look from one to the other of them, demanding their agreement – 'I know only too well how unreliable it can be. But the fact remains that that was all I had to go on then. A strong feeling that if I came here something might turn up.'

'Something that would help Harry Charlton,' said Meg, and 'Something that would involve you with "them",' said

Jenny, almost simultaneously, again using the description with perfect seriousness.

'Precisely,' Antony agreed. 'Uncle Nick saw what I meant too. He blew up at that point. Well, you can imagine.'

'Only what you expected, isn't it?'

'He'd been so damned forbearing up to then.'

Both Roger and Meg were looking puzzled. Jenny said, without much expression in her voice, 'Antony's worried about whether we ought to stay on in Kempenfeldt Square.'

'But you can't . . . you've been there for ever,' said Roger, aghast at this sudden and unexpected pronouncement. Meg was more reproachful.

'Darling, you're just being stupid,' she said.

Antony spread his hands in a wide, dissatisfied gesture, nearly spilling his sherry. 'I don't think so,' he told them. 'It isn't Vera I'm worried about, I think on the whole she quite likes having us around, but – '

Meg was still inclined to be indignant at what she regarded as an unreasonable attitude. Roger said, more sympathetically, 'You've got yourself in a proper muddle, haven't you?'

'I expect so.' Antony shrugged slightly, but the spectre was not to be so easily exorcised. 'The thought occurred to me once or twice during the summer – '

'It gave you no peace,' said Jenny, not argumentatively, but as one stating an incontrovertible fact.

' – but it was our disagreement over this business that really brought it to a head.'

'But Uncle Nick has always been . . . difficult,' Meg protested. 'Heaven knows, you don't always take him so seriously.'

'In the circumstances . . . it's no use talking about it,' said Antony. But it is quite likely that he would have gone on doing so if Roger, feeling it time to give his thoughts a more practical turn, hadn't come back into the conversation, saying thoughtfully:

'When you talked about relying on instinct you said that was all the reason you could offer . . . then.'

F 161

Before Antony could reply the waiter summoned them, and they went through into the restaurant itself, a much larger room though equally heavily panelled. Once more, the head waiter himself took them in charge, escorting them to a corner table at the opposite end of the room from the service door. Jenners' wasn't busy tonight, perhaps because it was the beginning of the week. Besides themselves there were only three couples in the room, all seated at a distance. Though even if all the tables had been full they were well spaced out, there'd have been no difficulty about talking privately.

Antony, who had manoeuvred himself into a seat with his back to the wall, accepted a large and rather ornate menu and waited until they were alone again. Then he put the menu down without consulting it and looked across at Roger, sitting opposite him. 'The answer to your question,' he said, 'is that, since I talked to Uncle Nick, something happened to make me feel that I am, after all, on the right track.'

'Something you haven't told Uncle Nick about,' said Jenny. Again there was no overt criticism in her tone, but her husband seemed to feel that something of the sort was implied.

'There really wasn't time for another row,' he said defensively. 'And the arrangement was already made. If I'd known then what I know now, Roger, I'd have suggested our coming alone. But Jenny didn't like the idea, she said I'd promised, and of course I had.'

'That's all very well,' said Meg, 'and of course Jenny was right. But what do you know, Antony, that makes you so cocksure all of a sudden? Don't keep us in suspense.'

'When I was changing before we came out I found this in my jacket pocket.' He took from his wallet a slip of paper, cut, from the looks of it, from an ordinary quarto sheet, and held it out so that Roger and Meg could see it. The message was in a rather spiky handwriting, not very easy to read: *Jenners' tonight at 8 o'clock, V.S.* 'It's nearly that time now,' he said.

'V.S.?' Meg was frowning.

162

'Vladimir Something,' said Roger. 'But I thought you said – '

'Solovki,' Antony interrupted him. 'And I was told he had gone back to Russia, but I think . . . I hope . . . that those are his initials.'

'This opens up a new train of thought,' said Roger slowly. 'Do you think after all the man in the crowd this morning didn't mean to harm you, just to deliver this?'

'I think this was a second string to his bow, for use if he failed in his primary purpose. I told you we spoke together for a moment, if he was deft enough about it I shouldn't have noticed him planting the note. And I can't think of any other opportunity anybody had.'

'No, I expect you're right. But what do you suppose he wants?' said Roger; a question that, in Antony's estimation, would have been very much better unasked. But while he was wondering how to word his reply, Jenny answered for him.

'It's a trap,' she said. 'It must be. Antony didn't give up his enquiries when Harry Charlton disappeared, so they want to kill him. He warned me what might happen, at least' – at this point, to Antony's relief, she smiled as though she were really amused – 'he said there might be some reaction. But that's what he meant.'

'If you've constituted yourself a bodyguard, Jenny – ' Roger began, but she shook her head at him.

'It's just that I don't like waiting at home while things are happening,' she said. 'Any more than Meg does. And for some reason,' she added, 'Antony has been much more reasonable than usual this last few days.'

'I don't think Uncle Nick would agree with you, love,' Maitland told her. Jenny turned to him quickly.

'I think you're wrong,' she said. 'He knows as well as I do that if there's any chance at all of helping Clare you're bound to take it. And if he didn't know it already, Vera would have told him.'

There was a small silence after that. Roger was staring at Jenny rather as though he had never seen her before, but she

163

had her serene look and met his gaze calmly. 'You agree with me, don't you, Meg?' she said, after a while.

'Of course I do.' Meg's agreement was emphatic. 'Don't worry so, Roger,' she went on. 'You never know, we may even be useful.'

Roger shrugged and gave Antony rather a helpless look. 'In that case I may as well change the subject,' he said in a resigned tone. 'Something that's puzzling me, Antony.'

'*You* don't believe me,' said Maitland, jumping immediately to the conclusion that pleased him least.

'It isn't that. If anyone ever had reason to trust you – '

'Now there's a word I don't care for,' said Antony gloomily. Roger gave him a look in which affection and exasperation were nicely blended.

'Put your mind to this, it may cheer you up,' he advised. 'Assuming – as I do – that all this is true, why was Harry Charlton framed in the first place? I mean, they went to considerable lengths, bribing at least one witness, whom they later found it convenient to dispose of; planting evidence in the studio – how was that done, incidentally?'

'By Meredith, when he was searching the place.'

'Yes, you said his involvement would explain a thing or two. They also paid a considerable sum into Charlton's Deposit Account . . . and stole one of his neckties, I was forgetting that. How was that done?'

'I don't see the difficulty about obtaining access to the studio. It would just be a matter of watching the place until both Charlton and Clare were out, and then picking the lock.'

'Easier said than done.'

'A basic skill in some professions,' Antony assured him, with an amused look at Meg, who had chosen this moment to remember her Presbyterian upbringing and was looking faintly shocked by his assertion. 'The front door of the studio isn't overlooked, which would make matters easier. I've been casting Meredith for that role, too, but of course I may be wrong about that. And I can pick a simple lock, Meg, if that's what you're thinking, but I haven't had occasion to do so for years.'

164

'I know, darling, not since you took to the law,' said Meg, giving him unexpectedly one of her more dazzling smiles.

'As for the larger question' – Roger had been quite right, the effort of concentration was having the effect of raising his spirits – 'it didn't occur to me straight away either, but I think the answer is a very simple one. It was a matter of protecting the real origin of the information the Russians were known to have, in expectation of further benefits from the same source. Framing Charlton emphasised Rickover's guilt . . . he admitted giving the basic information, but denied handing over any documents, remember?'

'But how did they know – ?'

'Rickover's confession was a piece of luck for "them", and given an opportunity like that they grabbed it with both hands. The idea was, as I see it, to prevent the authorities looking any further among the laboratory staff, and you must admit they succeeded admirably.'

'That makes sense,' said Roger. He realised as he spoke that Antony's eyes were no longer on him, but had become fixed on some point over his left shoulder. 'What is it? What's the matter?' he demanded urgently, but did not, to his credit, look round.

'There's a door I hadn't noticed in the panelling beside the service entrance,' said Antony. 'A man just came in.' All of a sudden his doubts and anxieties – even the unfamiliar anxiety of having involved Jenny and Meg in one of his enterprises – had vanished as if they had never been. 'Hold very tight, please,' he said, the Cockney accent as wickedly accurate as any mimicry he had ever indulged in, 'I think our party is about to be augmented.'

VI

He was right about that. The slight, dark man who had slipped through the hidden door made straight for their corner, halting only when he reached the space between Roger and Jenny,

165

and looking questioningly from one to the other of the two men. 'One of you must be Mr Maitland,' he said. 'The table was booked in that name.' His English was well nigh perfect, except for a slight tendency, which became apparent as the conversation progressed, to produce colloquialisms in inverted commas.

Maitland identified himself. His eyes were wary, but there was about him now an alertness, a sense of being worked up to a pitch of excitement, that must have been obvious, even to the newcomer. 'And you, I suppose,' he added, 'are V.S.'

'Vladimir Solovki, at your service.'

'Are you indeed?' That was said dryly.

'Very much so, though I realise you may take some convincing of that.' His eyes went curiously from Meg to Jenny. 'I didn't realise you would be throwing a party,' he said. There was some amusement in his voice, but to Antony at least it was obvious that he was as tense as a coiled spring.

'The arrangement was already made when I got your note.' Antony performed the introductions solemnly. 'I hope you are going to join us, Mr Solovki.'

'If Mrs Maitland will permit.' He waited for her murmured agreement before turning to signal imperiously to the waiter to bring up another chair. Roger and Jenny made room between them.

'Will you be wanting to order yet, Mr Solovki?' asked the waiter.

'Not just yet, I think.' But again his look deferred to Jenny. 'I suggest you bring us another round of drinks, and my usual, if you please.'

The waiter hurried off. Obviously there was something in Harry Charlton's theory that you got better service where you were known. 'Is Harry Charlton dead?' asked Maitland, dropping the words almost casually into the momentary silence that the man's departure left.

'On the contrary, he is very much alive . . . very angry,' Solovki told him. 'And he has broken his glasses, which makes it boring for him, not being able to read to pass the time. I am

166

here to invite you to visit him but I must warn you, the invitation is a trap.'

Jenny gave a gasp; whatever she was feeling she took no pleasure in having her prediction proved correct. Roger had turned to stare at the newcomer, and Antony's eyes never left his face. 'You're going to have to explain that,' said Meg, her affectations for the moment forgotten.

'Patience, Meg.' Maitland too seemed to have his own inner source of amusement. 'I feel sure our friend is about to explain himself. But first there is something else I should like to ask you, Mr Solovki. How does it come about that you are here? I was told you had gone back to Russia.'

'I have diplomatic immunity, you know. Or rather, I had, while I was still connected with the embassy. Still, it seemed a good idea to give out that I was no longer in the country. I have been staying here till a suitable opportunity arose to ship me home.'

The waiter returned at that point, and there was a pause until he had distributed glasses and left them alone again. 'Here?' said Maitland then on a note of enquiry. 'I saw you come into the restaurant just now. Where does that door lead?' If he found anything strange in the willingness with which Solovki answered his questions he gave no sign.

'The owner's apartment occupies the two floors above the restaurant,' Solovki told him readily. 'He has been here many years, a naturalised Englishman, and sometimes it is convenient to have a meeting place, or a place to put up visitors, which is *not* the embassy . . . because that, of course, is under observation.'

'I see. Is Charlton here?'

'He is.'

'Then I have just one more question for you, before we come to those explanations we spoke of. Did Harry Charlton pass on the information to you about the Fenton Laboratory project?' Roger caught the uncertainty in his voice and thought, but indulgently, all this talk and still he isn't sure. Jenny knew that already.

'He did not.' Again Solovki's reply came without hesitation. 'He would have made a very clumsy conspirator, you know, and in any case we weren't interested in such small fry as Jim Rickover.'

'Who then?'

'There was no need of an intermediary between the laboratory and ourselves. The information was given directly to someone rather older and wiser than myself by Vlasov's deputy, a man named Brewer.'

'Just as you said, darling,' said Meg in a congratulatory tone. Jenny sat quietly listening, as was her habit, but Antony had never been more aware of her presence. Roger said nothing either; he had taken out a notebook and pencil and was writing steadily. Solovki watched him for a moment, and again his expression was gently amused.

'You are wondering why I should spill the beans like this,' he asserted. 'Well, it is part of the explanation Mrs Farrell demanded of me. I want to stay in England, I want to ask for political asylum. So you see, I have been as much a prisoner here as Harry is.'

Even Meg was silenced by this announcement. Antony took his time before replying. 'That's a big step to take,' he said. 'How do we know you're telling the truth?'

'Because of the wholesale way in which I have given you the gen.' So far he had maintained a light tone, but now he became more serious. 'Because I assure you most solemnly,' he said, giving every word its full value, 'that I have come to hate our Communist regime. I have no relations to suffer for my sins . . . but you aren't interested in that. So I ask you, would I have told you all this, would I have admitted to you that the note I sent you was part of a plan – ?'

'You might,' said Jenny clearly, breaking her silence for the first time, 'if you knew we'd never be able to tell anybody else.'

Solovki turned to her quickly. You had, Antony considered, to admire his manner, a blend of the self-confident and the deferential. 'You are envisaging mass murder, Mrs Maitland.

Perhaps, when it comes, your dinner will be poisoned. I assure you, that would make too many difficulties for everybody. This place is useful, and Mr Derevenko's cover must not be broken.'

'But you had something in mind for my husband,' Jenny insisted stubbornly.

'That he should disappear, certainly, as Harry has disappeared. Not my idea, you understand, though I have pretended to go along with it. But it was not envisaged that so many of you would come here in answer to my note . . . no, you said the outing was arranged already when that was found. I must congratulate you on your discernment, Mr Maitland.'

'Never mind that. You say we must trust you, because you have warned me, and because you have allowed Mr Farrell to make certain notes, which will tend to confirm the story I have already given to the Special Branch. Let us suppose for a moment that I agree with you. The plan for my disposal has been spoiled by the presence of my wife and friends. What do you propose in its place?'

'Mr Derevenko – '

'The owner of this restaurant?'

'Yes. I was going to say that he has no idea you are not alone here. The waiters will do what he tells them, of course, but they do not know the real position. This very pleasant party you have organised will not have been reported to him. If you leave – preferably without waiting for your dinner – I can go with you and nothing will be said.'

'What about Harry Charlton?'

'That is where the snag comes in. When it is realised that I have gone he will not wait for orders. He will make for the embassy, and I think he will leave Harry's body behind him.'

'I see.' None of them interrupted him while he thought that out. 'Who else is in the apartment upstairs?' he asked at last. 'Besides Charlton and this Derevenko, I mean.'

'Tristan. You met him this morning.'

'And what is his function?'

'That's a little difficult to explain. But one thing will interest you, as I gather you have met the lady . . . he's Susan Brewer's brother.'

'With similar convictions to hers?'

'If you mean about politics, yes, of course. He's a Chartered Accountant, so Mr Derevenko tells me, does the books for this place, that's how they met.'

'And how does a Chartered Accountant come to be concerned . . . in this morning's caper, for instance?'

'He's on the payroll. You must see the advantages in having a native-born Englishman to take care of . . . jobs like that,' said Solovki, for the first time with a hint of embarrassment in his tone.

'As a matter of interest, did he mean to kill me?'

'Oh, yes, though even a spell in hospital would have been an advantage. An accident would have been much the best way . . . from their point of view, you know. The note was just in case anything went wrong, because when you started questioning people in the laboratory that was getting altogether too close to home. You couldn't be allowed to go on.'

'Was that why Charlton was kidnapped?'

'To discourage you, they hoped. But they kept him alive in case it became necessary to entice you here in the end.'

'Did Tristan kill the witness, Foster?'

'He did.'

'And arranged to suborn Meredith?'

'You have been busy. Meredith' – for the first time his pronunciation was at fault – 'Meredith had been useful before. In getting me out of the embassy, for instance. If it hadn't been for him I'd never have arrived here, of course. My mind was made up even then.'

Roger had been writing steadily. He looked up now and said, 'I can testify, and so can Meg, that Mr Solovki told you all this without prompting. When it's compared with what you told Wylie – '

'Too much of a coincidence to be anything but true. It should clear Harry Charlton, certainly, after the necessary

170

investigations have been made, but there's also the little matter of saving his life.'

That brought another silence. After a moment Jenny said, tentatively, 'If we go now perhaps we could get help before anything happens to him.'

'Just a minute, love. What sort of a man is this Derevenko?'

'Impulsive.'

'And Tristan?'

'Dangerous. I thought I'd made that clear.'

'How long will it be, do you suppose, before they realise you're not going back?'

'They must be wondering already why I haven't returned with you. It should have been so simple.' Solovki spread his hands. 'The quixotic Mr Maitland . . . your reputation is known, you see.' (Antony had a private grimace for that.) 'It was expected that as soon as you knew where Harry was you would rush to the rescue.'

'Yes, well – ' He was uncomfortable now, and when he broke off Roger came to the rescue.

'I think you're going to have to take what Mr Solovki says on trust, you know.'

'I think I must.' For the moment they might have been alone together. 'And the corollary of that is – '

'That we can't afford to go away and leave Charlton at the mercy of those two assassins upstairs.'

'Yes, but I think this is my job, don't you? If you go with Meg and Jenny – '

'No,' said Jenny, quite quietly.

'I'm with you there, darling,' said Meg approvingly.

'If you two are going to be difficult – '

'You've got to go,' said Roger. 'If I'm right in what Antony's planning, you're the most important part of the operation. I'll stay, of course.'

Jenny's eyes met Meg's in consultation, then she turned back to her husband again. 'All right,' she said.

'All right then, here's what we'll do.' Suddenly Maitland

171

was decisive. 'Give Meg your notebook, Roger. Go straight back to Kempenfeldt Square, the pair of you, and find Uncle Nick. Take Mr Solovki with you. I'm afraid you won't be able to get your coat, Mr Solovki,' he added, 'and I think there's one of your people in the street. He'll be – where would I be in similar circumstances? – across the street, he has to be. So you'd better forget your manners and let Jenny – she's tallest – walk on the outside of the pavement. Keep your head turned away as though you're talking to Meg on your other side, that should give you some protection even if the chap knows you by sight.'

'If I am to put these charming ladies into danger – '

'It's nothing to the danger they'd be in if they stayed here,' said Maitland bluntly. He was nowhere near so sure as Solovki seemed to be that the unknown Mr Derevenko would draw the line at mass murder.

'Very well.'

'But what am I to do with him?' asked Jenny, with something a little plaintive in her tone.

Antony turned back to her, and just for a moment a feeling of gratitude submerged every other emotion. He didn't know what he'd have done if she'd argued. 'Take him home with you, love,' he said. 'Uncle Nick can advise him on his problem as well as anybody I know. But before you go into that, tell him what's happened here, how everything we've heard confirms what I told him this afternoon, and ask him to see if he can get in touch with Wylie. He'll get some action, if anybody can. We need help, and we need it fast. Is there another way into the upstairs apartment?' he added, turning to Solovki.

'Yes, of course. From Blackhorse Street, number twenty-nine.'

'A back entrance?'

'Only through the kitchen of the restaurant.'

Meg was tucking away the notebook in her handbag. Solovki was already on his feet. Jenny said, with the first sign of uncertainty she had shown, 'What are you going to do?'

172

'I think we shall wait a quarter of an hour or so, to give you a chance to set things in motion. After that . . . will you tell the waiter as you leave, Mr Solovki, that we have an appointment with the proprietor at nine o'clock, then we can go upstairs when the time comes without occasioning too much surprise.'

'I'll do that. But – ' It was his turn now to look uneasy. Now the time had come, the final step . . . Antony found himself wholeheartedly believing for the first time in the young Russian's honesty of intention. 'How will he receive me, this relative of yours?'

'If you're sincere, he'll help you.'

'I am sincere, but . . . I am not an important person, you know, who knows many secrets. Some things I can tell' – his English was becoming more stilted as he grew more nervous – 'but nothing of any great moment.'

'That can't be helped. Look here, you must have thought all this out before you joined us.'

'Of course, it is a decision of many months.'

'All right then.' He held the Russian's eyes for a long moment, then Solovki turned away, shrugging, and began to cross the room to where the head waiter was standing. 'Go with him, you two,' Antony went on. 'Your part in this is the hardest one, you know.'

'Uncle Nick is not an ogre,' said Meg, who had always borne his strictures with equanimity. She shared a smile impartially between her husband and his friend. 'I shall be with Jenny, we'll expect you in an hour or so.'

But Jenny had still a word to say. She looked at Antony and saw again the blaze of excitement that had seized him, though briefly, earlier in the day. Roger, too, had cheered perceptibly at the prospect of action. 'I don't want to – to throw a spanner in the works,' she told them, 'but when you said, "after that", Antony, what did you mean?'

'We shall go upstairs, love.'

'But what can you *do*?'

Roger began to laugh. 'You know the answer to that perfectly well, Jenny,' he told her cheerfully.

'What is it then?'

'He'll talk.'

VII

Jenny, fortunately, had seen the funny side of that. She had accompanied Meg and Vladimir Solovki composedly, smiling an apology at the rather puzzled waiter as she went, and only revealing by the fact that she turned in the doorway for a last look at the corner table that her mind was not completely at rest.

The minutes went by slowly after that. Once Antony said, 'I suppose we were right to trust Solovki.'

'I don't think we had much choice.'

'Harry Charlton liked him,' said Antony worriedly. 'And so did Clare. But I mean . . . Jenny and Meg.'

'I know what you mean. They should be home by now.'

Antony thought about that, and found it comforting. All the same, as the time dragged by his excitement began to fade, to be replaced by a more familiar chill of apprehension. And because he could talk to Roger, or nearly, he said into the silence, 'I wonder just what Solovki meant by impulsive.'

Roger, who had moved to Jenny's chair and could now see the length of the room almost as well as Antony could, said softly, 'I think we're about to find out.'

Maitland looked up. A square-built man of about sixty, very expensively tailored, had come out of the hidden door and was looking round in a rather bewildered way. The head waiter went up to him, they spoke for a moment together, and then the newcomer was coming across the room. Seeing his eyebrows, which were perhaps his most marked characteristic, Roger had just time to murmur, 'Brezhnev in person,' before he came alongside. Antony's answering smile was a little absent-minded, his attention was already concentrated upon

174

the square-built man as absolutely as it might have been upon a witness in court.

'I do not understand what I am told. That I make an appointment for nine o'clock. I know nothing of this.'

'Not the actual time, perhaps, but I understood you wanted to see me. My name's Maitland,' Antony explained. 'I came, after all, by invitation. That is, if you are Mr Derevenko.'

'That is my name.' In spite of the years he was reputed to have spent in England, he did not speak the language with the grace of his younger fellow-countryman. 'But if you are Mr Maitland,' he said, and now he spoke with a sort of grudging politeness, 'where is my young friend, Vladimir, who was to have brought you to me?'

'There was an errand he wished to do.' Antony spoke casually, and watched the heavy eyebrows that Roger had commented on draw together in a quite fearsome frown.

'He had no leave.' But he pulled himself up there and turned his rather lowering regard on Roger. 'And this gentleman?' he said.

'Roger Farrell, a friend of mine.' Antony's tone was negligent. 'He is as interested as I am in what has happened to Harry Charlton.'

'That very tedious young man. Vladimir has told you he is here?'

Antony smiled and Roger, watching him, could almost have sworn it was with real amusement. 'You haven't found him an acceptable guest?' he asked sympathetically. And continued, before Derevenko could reply, 'Never mind, we've come to take him off your hands, you know.'

It was the Russian's turn to smile. Both of his companions had the same thought . . . they liked him much better without it. 'Come upstairs with me to my apartment and you shall see him,' he promised.

'Yes, that might be best.' Maitland got up as he spoke. 'I am quite aware of your present intentions towards us, Mr Derevenko,' he added, with no change of tone, 'but I think when you have heard what I have to say you may think it wise to reconsider them. So, if I may presume to advise you, I shouldn't do anything rash.'

That brought a long look from Derevenko, before he turned and led the way across the room. The lights in the restaurant were dim, but beyond the door it was bright enough. A passage on their left led to what was presumably the door on to Blackhorse Street that Solovki had spoken of; where they stood the hall was wider and to their right a solid-looking staircase ascended to the upper floor. Their host stood aside to let them pass. 'If you will precede me,' he invited.

Antony took the lead. Now that it came to the point he wasn't quite sure what he expected to find; still less was he certain how he was going to put in the time until the earliest possible moment for help to arrive. The easiest thing would be to convince Derevenko that the game was up, something on the lines of 'fly at once, all is discovered,' if, of course, that could be done without precipitating wholesale carnage. But every instinct rebelled against taking that course, because if Derevenko and the man called Tristan once made it to the Russian embassy you might as well say goodbye to any hope of bringing them to justice. All the same, his first responsibility was the saving of life ('Your own would be one of them,' a voice in his head told him mockingly); it might not be possible to make justice the only criterion.

Roger, who had more confidence in his friend's ingenuity than Maitland had in himself, trod in his footsteps hopefully. If his imagination was less vivid than Antony's, he was nobody's fool and had assessed long since the difficulties and dangers that lay ahead. But where danger was concerned it was his nature to take things as they came, and certainly Derevenko, crowding on his heels, could not have guessed that he was alert to any hint that action might be called for.

The staircase led straight into a big living-room, and here again the passion for panelling that had been so evident in the restaurant had been given play. But it was a pleasant room, very masculine in its furnishings, with bookcases, deep leather chairs, a big high-polished desk in one corner, and bowls of

176

tawny chrysanthemums placed at strategic points. Which made Antony wonder at once, irrelevantly, about his host's domestic arrangements. But he had no time to pursue this fascinating byway. In one of the chairs, backing on to the desk, sat Harry Charlton, looking strangely defenceless without his glasses; At first glance he appeared to be sitting comfortably enough, but when he raised his hands by way of greeting Antony saw that they were bound together. It took a further look to see that his ankles, too, were tied. Uncharacteristically, he didn't immediately say anything, though he managed a rather lop-sided grin, but his eyes moved deliberately, so that Maitland, following their direction, saw for the first time the man he had encountered in South Ealing that morning. Tristan's rather boyish face had now a grim, wary look, and he had them covered. A revolver, not a make Antony was familiar with, but he thought he had never seen a more deadly-looking weapon. That he had been expecting it didn't make him like it any better.

He paused a few paces into the room to let Roger come up beside him, threw a warning look in Charlton's direction (though he wasn't sure what that young man could distinguish the niceties of expression without his glasses) and addressed the man with the gun directly. 'I'm sure you're anxious to finish off what you started this morning, but circumstances have changed since then. I think you'd better hear what I have to say first.'

'I don't understand.' Tristan's eyes sought his principal, but the revolver remained steady. He looked what Solovki had called him, dangerous, and Antony wondered how he could have had so different an impression of him earlier in the day. 'Where is Vladimir, and who is this other man?'

'A Mr Farrell,' said Derevenko, who seemed to have an incurable urge towards politeness. 'As for Vladimir's absence, that is something Mr Maitland is going to explain to us. So for the present, no shooting; unless, of course, it becomes absolutely necessary.'

By this time whatever instinct of caution had held Harry

177

Charlton silent had obviously worn off. 'How on earth did you get here?' he demanded. 'I'm glad to see you, of course, but I don't see how you managed it.'

'It's a long story.' It was only to be expected that Harry's first words would form a question. 'I'll tell you some time, but just now I'm more interested in what happened to you.'

'Tell me first, how is Clare?'

'Staying with us. Safe and sound, but not very happy. However, perhaps we can remedy that.'

'I shouldn't count on it.' Whether or not he realised that Maitland's purpose was to squander as much time as possible, Harry was playing up splendidly. 'This chap told me' – he jerked his head in Tristan's direction – 'that they were only keeping me alive until you got here. Sort of using me as bait.'

'This is to waste time.' Derevenko had come past them into the room. Beside him Antony, who knew his friend very well, could sense Roger's seething impatience; if it hadn't been for the gun, still trained steadily on Maitland, he could have tackled the Russian as he went.

'You must forgive us.' It was inevitable that Antony should mimic their host's rather heavy-handed politeness. 'It's your own doing, you know, that we've so much catching up to do.' He saw that the phrase puzzled Derevenko and added kindly, 'Catching up on our news, I mean.'

'I doubt if Charlton knows what happened,' said Tristan. He spoke harshly, and again Antony wondered at the different impression he had had of him earlier. The sort of man, obviously, who would melt into the landscape at will, and a jolly useful accomplishment too.

'Then perhaps you will fill me in.' He thought it must be as clear to them as it was to himself that he was playing for time, but neither Derevenko nor Tristan seemed to have any fault to find with the suggestion. Perhaps they hoped to demonstrate their complete control of the situation.

'He went for a walk. I think he was probably making for that pub he's so fond of, but he never got there. A quiet street, the prick of a needle, a car waiting – '

'That's quite a lyrical description,' said Harry approvingly. 'It all adds up to the fact that I woke up here.'

'And would have been dead by now,' said Tristan, 'if you, Mr Maitland, had taken the hint and refrained from further meddling.'

'You ought to meet my uncle, you'd find yourself in complete sympathy with him,' said Antony. 'That's how he always refers to those of my activities of which he disapproves.' All the time they were speaking he was conscious of Derevenko's silence. Tristan's might be the hand on the gun, but it was the older man who was unquestionably in command. And even as he thought this he became aware that Roger had shifted his position slightly. 'Not until we've tried everything,' he said, not looking round. He didn't need to, he was sure enough that the other man would back up his tactics. The time might come, of course – he was practically certain that it would – when action became inevitable; when it did, they would act together. And probably both get killed, his mind added as a cheerless corollary to that. But there was no time now for such thoughts.

Derevenko seemed to have decided to take a hand again. If he found the meaning of his enemy's last remark obscure, he gave no sign. 'I really must insist, Mr Maitland, that you give me the explanation I asked for,' he said, and Antony, turning his attention to him again thought he saw for the first time exactly what Solovki had meant. This was a man poised on the edge of violence, whose decisions would be sudden, and from which there would be no appeal. 'Where is Vladimir?' asked Derevenko softly. And now Maitland judged it was no longer time to temporise, at least, not quite so obviously.

'Didn't I tell you?' His air of surprise was nicely done. 'We made a party up to come here tonight . . . such an excellent restaurant, I really do congratulate you.'

'Who?' Derevenko's tone was in itself a warning.

'Mr Farrell and I. My wife, and his wife. It's quite simple really. Solovki is escorting the ladies home. That's why I told you to think twice before you started anything. Our presence

179

here is known. If you're planning two more disappearances – '

'Four of you!' said Tristan a little wildly. Antony proceeded to emphasise his point, and Roger, listening, wondered whether Derevenko recognised the faintly mocking tone of his mimicry.

'I'm sorry, of course, to make things inconvenient for you, but you can see that anything in the way of – of a mass execution would cause comment, to say the least.'

It is certain that his words gave Tristan to think. He wasn't so sure of their effect on the impulsive Mr Derevenko until he turned his eyes on the Russian and realised that he was struggling with an idea.

'You are confusing me, Mr Maitland,' Derevenko complained, catching his look. 'You have said you knew my intentions towards you. Why then did you let your two companions leave the restaurant with one of your enemies for escort?'

'I've already told you. I don't think you can afford too many unexplained deaths.' Antony did his best to give the *non sequitur* a specious ring.

'No, I think there is some other reason.' Derevenko had a calculating look. He's getting there, thought Maitland, the point I wanted to avoid, though how I could have expected . . . 'You know altogether too much, Mr Maitland. What did Vladimir say to you?'

'That Harry Charlton was here.'

'Yes . . . yes . . . that was the arrangement.' Derevenko brushed the information aside impatiently.

'As for the rest, it wasn't too difficult a conundrum really. Solovki merely confirmed what we already knew.'

'He is a traitor then.'

'I suppose he is, from your point of view.' There was nothing for it now, if he didn't speak they could be dead within seconds. Save something from the wreckage then, their lives at least . . . if he could. 'I know, for instance – and I informed the authorities of it this afternoon – that Jim Rickover was not the source of the information about the Fenton Laboratory project. It was a much more senior member of the staff,

Vincent Brewer. So you see, if you kill us it won't convince anybody of Charlton's guilt, which I suppose is the best reason you could have for doing so. And whatever scheme you had for disposing of our bodies, don't flatter yourself you'll have time to carry it out.'

'It would be a great personal satisfaction to leave you dead,' said Tristan viciously.

'I am inclined to agree with you.' There was no mistaking the gleam in Derevenko's eye, it was one of pure hatred. 'It would be a puzzle for the police – '

'No puzzle at all.' Maitland's interruption at last was urgent, no longer the polished tone that reflected his enemy's manner. The final throw, and he was too uncertain of the outcome to maintain completely the appearance of detachment. 'You haven't been listening to a word I say,' he complained. 'I told you I spoke to the Special Branch this afternoon, and when I did I gave them every bit of information that I had, including the fact that this place was being used' – will he recognise that for a lie? – 'and by the time Solovki has confirmed what I had to say they'll be ready to take action.'

It wasn't working. There was death in Derevenko's face. Not the slightest movement betrayed Roger's tension, but Antony was aware of it and knew that his friend had read their sentence too. He took a deep breath and said deliberately, 'So the quicker you're out of here – '

That was when Roger made his move. His first action was to grab Antony's arm – luckily he had been standing on his left – and swing him with all his force out of the line of fire. That done – it seemed to Maitland that it was all in one quick movement – he took two strides to place himself behind Derevenko, gripping his arms, so that by the time the revolver swung round the Russian's body formed a shield between himself and danger.

It was at this point that the plan began to go astray. It had been Roger's intention to use Derevenko as a projectile – an ambitious programme with so solid a man – shoving him violently in the direction of the man with the gun; and thus

181

effectively distracting Tristan's attention for a few, vital moments that could be put to good use by two determined men. But whether or not he sensed what was in his enemy's mind, the Russian foiled him neatly, falling back heavily on his assailant so that for a few valuable seconds Roger was fully occupied in trying to sustain his weight.

If Antony had lost his balance, that would have been stalemate. He staggered a little, but the sudden action had distracted Tristan's attention, as well it might, and before the gun was trained on Maitland again he threw himself forward. The revolver went off harmlessly as his left shoulder connected with Tristan's body somewhere below the belt. For the moment he was on top, but that couldn't last, of course. Even as he tried to lift his hand to pin down the other man's arm he was aware of the agony that any violent motion started up in his shoulder . . .

And then there was Roger's voice. He sounded a little breathless, but quite calm. 'It's all right, Antony, you can get up now. I've got the gun.' And as Maitland dragged himself up, painfully, there came from a distance the sound of somebody hammering urgently on a door.

Antony stood for a moment surveying the scene, and waiting for the waves of nausea to subside. Roger had backed up beside Harry Charlton's chair, looking very much as though he had been born with a revolver in his hand. He was covering Derevenko, who seemed to have been thrown aside as unceremoniously as Maitland himself had been, but who was now scrambling again to his feet. 'You'd better keep your henchman in check,' Roger told him, 'because if he tries anything . . . or if you do yourself, for that matter – you're the one who is going to get shot.' No one listening to him could have doubted for a moment that he meant what he said. 'I think that knocking is coming from downstairs, Antony,' he added. 'Hadn't you better see who it is?'

'It can't be Wylie yet,' said Antony. But he did not say it with much conviction.

Tristan must have been winded, he hadn't yet picked him-

182

self up from the floor. Harry Charlton, whose existence Maitland had almost forgotten in spite of his being the cause of all the trouble, said in a commendably level voice, 'You might untie me first. I'm damned uncomfortable, you know.'

'Shall I?' For the moment Antony felt incapable of even so small a decision, and was glad to look to Roger for guidance.

'If you're quick about it. And don't – ' But Maitland was already moving behind Derevenko to reach Harry's chair.

'That isn't the first time you've dealt violently with a situation, you and your friend,' said Charlton, as he started to struggle with the knots. The cords had been pulled tight, and must have been extremely painful. 'It would be interesting to know – ' But even Harry was silenced when he took a good look at his rescuer.

By the time Antony walked down the stairs a few minutes later, leaving Roger still in command of the situation and Charlton massaging his sore wrists, the knocking had become almost demented. It must have been audible in the restaurant, but the door remained shut; a matter of discipline, perhaps, or perhaps Derevenko had locked it behind him. Antony stepped past it to the more imposing door, the one he supposed opened on to Blackhorse Street, and fumbled for a moment with a rather complicated system of locks and bolts. The hammering continued in a frenzied crescendo, but he had it open at last.

There seemed to be a crowd of people in the street outside, but he had eyes for only two of them. Wylie he couldn't very well miss, he was right in front of him with his hand still raised to the knocker; nor could he help seeing the taller figure of his uncle, elbowing the Special Branch man to one side with a quite uncharacteristic lack of formality.

'You will oblige me, Antony,' said Sir Nicholas awfully, 'by telling me who has been killed.'

TUESDAY, 19th OCTOBER

I

'They'd heard the shot, you see,' said Antony, many hours later, 'so naturally – '

'He was anxious about you both,' said Jenny, sounding for once very sure of herself. Her husband shook is head at her.

'He was furious,' he said sombrely, setting the record straight. 'But I have to admit I was pleased to see him for all that. And Wylie too. But I still don't understand how they got there so quickly.'

They had got back at dawn, Sir Nicholas, Roger, Harry Charlton and Antony, to find their womenfolk awaiting them in the study at Kempenfeldt Square. The odd thing was – though this didn't occur to Antony until later – that both Gibbs and Mrs Stokes were still in attendance, the one producing beer, which he must have purloined from the Maitlands' quarters, and the other a profusion of sandwiches, very welcome to the younger men after an evening's fasting. After the scratch meal was over Harry and Clare had gone back to the studio, both of them, with the resilience of youth, seeming to have recovered completely from the terrors of the last few days; but the others, on being informed quite clearly by Sir Nicholas that their presence was no longer required, had repaired upstairs to mull over the night's affairs, 'Because, darlings,' as Meg said, not at all sleepily, 'I've a rehearsal at ten, and there just isn't time to go to bed.'

Now she was sitting near Jenny on the sofa, while Roger had Sir Nicholas's chair and Antony was standing in his favourite place with his back to the newly-lighted fire. 'It's all quite simple,' said Meg, enjoying the explanation. 'We brought Mr Solovki here – he said we should call him

185

Vladimir – and we told Uncle Nick and Vera exactly what you said. So he tried to ring Inspector Wylie but that was no good, so he just took off by himself.'

'That doesn't explain . . . what happened to Solovki, anyway? He wasn't here when we got back.'

'After Uncle Nick phoned,' said Jenny, 'to say everything was all right but that you'd probably be delayed, somebody called and took him away. I think it was somebody Inspector Wylie sent. And I hope everything will be all right, Antony, because I do think he was sincere.'

'That's his problem, love.' But he added, when he saw her anxious look, 'I think after all that happened this evening . . . well, I don't know, of course, but I dare say *you'd* be able to persuade Uncle Nick to put in a good word for him. That is,' he added doubtfully, 'if a sponsor does any good in a case like this.'

'Don't worry, Jenny,' said Roger, who could not bear, any more than Antony could, to see her without the serene look that was so much a part of her. 'I've a sort of feeling that Charlton's right about his friend, Vladimir. And if he is, we aren't the only people who'll realise it.'

'I suppose not.' If Jenny wasn't convinced, she still made a good attempt at putting the problem behind her. 'To get back to what you were asking, Antony, I don't understand any more than you do how Inspector Wylie got to Blackhorse Street.'

'I can tell you that,' said Roger. 'And so could Antony if he hadn't been too preoccupied with the explanations he had to make to take in what was being said to him. You know he said he thought there was one of "them" outside the restaurant.' They had all adopted Jenny's word as being as expressive as any other.

'I knew we were being followed on the way there,' said Antony apologetically. For some reason Roger seemed momentarily confused by the admission.

'Yes . . . well . . . it happened to be one of Wylie's chaps. Derevenko, I suppose, relied on Vladimir's good offices to get you into his clutches. But the Special Branch man got a bit confused when Jenny and Meg left with Solovki; so he got in touch with Wylie, and the Inspector and Uncle Nick met on the doorstep.'

'It still seems to me,' said Meg (playing Portia, as Antony might have said) 'that there's a lot to be done in this case.'

'Not my job,' said Antony, and for the first time there was some satisfaction evident in his voice. 'But I'm not worried about that really. Derevenko and Tristan – what *is* his other name, I wonder? – have a case against them for kidnapping at the very least, and I expect the rest will follow. Solovki's evidence will clear Harry Charlton and go a long way towards convicting the Brewers and the renegade Special Branch man, Meredith. Anyway, Wylie promised those three would be arrested – I do remember that much, Roger – and once that is done Basil can complete his project at leisure . . . Meg, if Jenny lends you a nightgown, won't you go to bed after all for an hour or two? We'll all be dead tomorrow.'

'You mean today,' said Meg, who looked as lively as ever. But perhaps she saw that he had had about as much as he could take for the time being, because she glanced at her husband and then got up in a determined way. 'It isn't worth going to bed, but we'll have to change before we can face the day so I think we'd better go home now. I'm glad you succeeded in saving each other's lives, darlings,' she added, dividing a smile between Roger and Antony. And then, in the gentle tone that Antony had never heard her use to anybody but his wife, 'Good night, Jenny. There's nothing for you to worry about any longer, you know.'

'And that's true enough,' said Antony, when he came back from seeing the Farrells out. 'Not that there was much life saving about my part in the affair, but still – '

Jenny made no reply to that, except to say after a moment, 'We may as well go to bed, anyway.' She was thinking: If you weren't worrying, Antony, I needn't either. But he was, and she knew it. All the same, she did not speak her thought aloud.

They slept until lunch time and, after they had eaten, Antony went into chambers, leaving Jenny to make whatever arrangements she deemed necessary for the usual Tuesday night's entertaining. Sir Nicholas was missing, and not even old Mr Mallory knew where he had gone; an unprecedented state of affairs, but not unwelcome to Maitland that afternoon.

He walked home. Not that he was particularly early, but the fit of restlessness was still upon him. Gibbs was in the hall when he let himself in, to glare his disapproval of such tardiness and inform him that Sir Nicholas and Lady Harding were already with Mrs Maitland. They'd never persuade Gibbs to retire, now that he seemed to have taken such a fancy to Vera. And that was something else he'd been wrong about: he had thought she wouldn't take kindly to having things done for her, might even feel diffident about giving orders, but now for the first time in memory his uncle's household seemed to be running on an even keel. But then he remembered that it might not make any difference to him or to Jenny whether Gibbs stayed or went.

Everything looked as usual when he went into the living-room. An October evening that had turned cold, so that the fire was welcome, with the curtains drawn already against the encroaching darkness and the lamplight gilding Jenny's hair. It was all as dear to him as it was familiar, but the problem was still to be faced.

Jenny got up to give him sherry, and he put the glass down in its accustomed place near the clock and turned to look down at his family. Sir Nicholas had his normal, leisured air; Vera – and that was odd – an unaccustomed wariness; while Jenny, who had maintained her serenity so well during the last troubled days, was worried again. For which he blamed himself, she had always been sensitive to his moods. With some idea of reassuring her he said into the silence, 'Everything back to normal again,' but the words sounded tentative, and he could not tell how any of his audience received them.

'As normal as they ever are,' said Sir Nicholas. There was no malice behind the words, but Jenny saw her husband flinch and said hurriedly:

'What's going to happen to Harry Charlton?'

Sir Nicholas turned to her. 'He will have to stand trial, of course, on the lesser charge of wrongfully obtaining official information which might be of use to an enemy. And I have no doubt,' he added caustically, 'that your husband will put forward a telling argument on his behalf.'

'Nothing to it,' said Vera, thinking perhaps that some encouragement was in order. 'Do it on your head.' And then, with a return to her usual gruffness of manner, 'Alive, isn't he? Ought to be grateful to you.'

'That's Roger's doing, not mine.' Antony was rather determinedly casual, he had no desire to arouse any memories of the previous night. 'But in all the circumstances . . . am I being too optimistic, Uncle Nick?'

'If you ask me,' said Sir Nicholas with the flicker of a smile, 'Mr Charlton has got his story and doesn't care much for anything else. Even though he won't be able to publish anything about the reason for all the trouble – '

Jenny and Vera exchanged an amused look. 'You're wrong there, Uncle Nick,' Jenny told him. 'About his not caring for anything else, I mean. Clare rang up today.'

'That does not surprise me. What had she to say?'

'You remember when everything was awful for Harry she said she'd marry him, and then he was the one who was unwilling. Well, now he's holding her to it, Clare said he's quite determined. So she agreed.'

'Very proper.' Sir Nicholas was approving. 'We may take it then that Mr Charlton's estimate of his own prospects tallies pretty well with ours.'

'Whatever he is, he's certainly no pessimist,' said Antony thoughtfully. 'And I'm sure of one thing, he wouldn't do anything he felt was going to hurt Clare.' He was nerving himself for the question he knew must be asked sooner or later, because whatever the result was it would be better than all this uncertainty, but before he could continue Jenny broke in.

'There's one thing that makes me simply furious,' she said, with a very un-Jenny-like venom in her tone. 'That man Briggs – '

'I think I may say that I share your feelings to some extent.' Sir Nicholas was at his blandest. 'So I took it upon myself to visit the Chief Superintendent at Scotland Yard today.'

'Uncle Nick, you didn't!'

'Have I ever given you occasion, Antony, to doubt my word?'

'No, of course not, but – ' Antony was confused. The conversation seemed to be tending in the direction he had designed, but now he wasn't sure that was what he wanted. 'I know you hate it when I have . . . well . . . a disagreement with the police,' he concluded lamely.

'The word disagreement is not one I should have chosen in this instance,' said his uncle consideringly. 'However' – he smiled – 'I do not think you will have any further trouble in that quarter; not for a month or two, at least. And even then, if you could contrive to keep out of mischief – ' He did not attempt to complete the sentence, but sat looking up placidly at his nephew. And suddenly Antony laughed, though a trifle ruefully.

'That takes me back,' he said.

'To the days when you had some respect for my views, perhaps,' enquired Sir Nicholas gently.

'Something like that. Look here – ' He glanced at Vera and then back to his uncle again. 'No,' he said decisively, 'it will wait.'

Sir Nicholas scowled at him. 'If you have something to say to me, Antony – '

He might not have responded to that, it was Vera who turned the scale in favour of candour. 'Get it out in the open,' she advised. 'Been acting like a cat on hot bricks ever since we got home.' Something in the simple way she said that encouraged him in his belief that she, at least, was satisfied with the *status quo*. But there was still Sir Nicholas to consider.

'Look here, Uncle Nick,' he said again; not an auspicious beginning. 'It's just that we were wondering, Jenny and I – all right then, love, *I* was wondering – whether you and Vera would like to have the place to yourselves.'

Vera began, 'The last thing I want to do – ' But she broke off there. Perhaps she realised that this was something that must be resolved between uncle and nephew.

'You will remember, of course,' said Sir Nicholas, and again his tone was reflective, 'that the arrangement was intended from the beginning to be a temporary one.' Vera moved uneasily at his words, and he held up a hand as though he suspected she was about to interrupt him. 'No, my dear, let me finish. As far as I am concerned, however, I have long regarded our way of life as permanent. If your reading of the situation, Antony, is different from mine, there is nothing I can do to stop you leaving.' He paused there and there was a moment's silence, in which Antony realised, with unpleasant clarity, that everything hung on the next sentence. 'I should be sorry, however,' said Sir Nicholas disagreeably, 'to lose Jenny's company.'

Antony looked at him. Borrowing his uncle's manner, for once in his life quite consciously, he replied in kind. 'I should, of course, regret inconveniencing you in any way.' Then he moved quickly, pulling Jenny to her feet and giving her an enthusiastic hug. 'It's all right, love,' he told her. 'We're staying!'